HIDDEN MICKEY
ADVENTURES 3

THE MERMAID'S TALE

[signature]

By

Nancy Temple Rodrigue

2014

DOUBLE-R BOOKS

Disclaimer

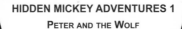

ACKNOWLEDGEMENTS

I WOULD LIKE TO THANK THE FOLLOWING PEOPLE
FOR HELPING ME BRING THIS NOVEL TO LIFE:

JIM KORKIS, AUTHOR OF *VAULT OF WALT*
FOR HIS HELP WITH THE SUBMARINE LAGOON, WALT'S
FEDORA AND THE CLADDAGH RINGS

SAM GENNAWEY, AUTHOR OF *THE DISNEYLAND STORY*
FOR HIS HELP WITH DISNEY TIMELINES

PATTY GRIGGS
FOR SHARING HER IDEA FOR GRANDMA MARGARET

TIMOTHY CRUMRINE
FOR THE HISTORY ON *THE LITTLE MERMAID*

SUSAN MURPHY
FOR HER VIDEO OF MAIN STREET ADDRESSES

J. C. TREGARTHEN
FOR HIS HELP WITH THE MAIN STREET BUILDINGS

THANKS AND ACKNOWLEDGEMENTS ALSO GO TO
OUR PROOFREADERS AND EDITORS:

LAURA ELIZABETH O'LACY, M.H.S.

KIMBERLEE KEELINE, ENGLISH, PH.D.
WWW.KEELINE.COM

Dear Readers,

Walt Disney's interest in mermaids was long-standing. Soon after he finished production on Snow White in 1937, he wanted to dive into Hans Christian Andersen's tale of the Little Mermaid. However, the project had to be shelved—much to Walt's regret. Flash forward to the 1980's when The Disney Company was animating the version we love so dearly. Miraculously, Walt's original script for *The Little Mermaid* was found. What was interesting was that some of Walt's changes to the original storyline were the same as the changes made by the later Disney writers.

Hidden Mickey Adventures 3: The Mermaid's Tale begins shortly after Peter and Catie find the mermaid hidden in the Haunted Mansion at Disneyland. At the home of Catie's grandmother Margaret, they find a familiar gray capsule buried in the attic. But, more importantly, they find out something fascinating about Margaret—she had been one of the mermaids swimming in the Submarine Lagoon in the 1960's.

In this fun-filled novel, we examine some of the attractions that have been gone from Disneyland for many years. Relive the original Submarine Voyage and the Motor Boat Cruise. Stand with Walt himself on the deck of the Chicken of the Sea Pirate Ship. Get reacquainted with the mysterious Blonde-Haired Man who worked side-by-side with Walt in the original novel *Hidden Mickey: Sometimes Dead Men Do Tell Tales!*

Our favorite security guard Wolf is always nearby as a new villain threatens the children. She has her own Mermaid's Tale to complete and is fanatically dedicated to seeing it through to the bitter end—even if it means going through Wolf to do it. There is something unsettling about her that he can't put a finger on and he finds that he may have bitten off more than he can chew!

Enjoy the history of Disneyland and the new adventure,

Nancy Temple Rodrigue

Prologue

The mermaid was surprisingly light as Peter removed her from her hiding place. She had been hid in one of the chests placed around the attic scene in Disneyland's Haunted Mansion. As he tested the weight and guessed she was made out of wood, he could hear the dull thud of something loose inside the body. Only about sixteen inches long, her arms were at her sides as if she was swimming. Catie's flashlight played over the mermaid's light green tail. Her long red hair was carved to look as if it was flowing back over her shoulders.

"She's so pretty! Are those pearls attached? They don't look like the rest of her."

"No, they're separate. Look here, Catie. There's another set of pearls under these that cover her…uh…chest. They looked carved. Wonder why there are two. Hey, do you think she's supposed to be Ariel? She has red hair."

Catie wasn't sure. "Her face is all wrong for Ariel. This doesn't look like a real mermaid." At Peter's laugh, she quickly defended herself. "You know what I mean! This looks too…too old, I guess. Like the other stuff in the room."

Before they could continue their discussion, they both heard a noise in the far corner of the room. When they shined their flashlights to investigate, they were shocked to see the same woman who had watched them from the gate.

"Put the mermaid down." The order was clear as she moved closer, her hand going into the huge purse at her side. "That doesn't belong to you."

"Who are you? How did you get in here?" Peter stepped in front of Catie and handed her the mermaid behind his back. He could feel her fumble with his backpack as she tried to cram it inside. *Good girl, Catie.* Even though he put on a brave front, his heart pounded in his chest as he faced this very angry woman.

"Don't you question me, boy. I saw you sneak in here and followed you. You aren't the only one who knows how to pick a lock."

"I didn't pick the lock. I have a key! And that means you don't work here and don't belong!"

A smug smile came over the woman's face. She looked to be in her early forties. "A key, huh? I might just have to take that away from you."

"I'd like to see you try!"

"Peter, don't make her madder." Catie had gotten the mermaid stuffed into his pack and began to panic. "We have to get out of here!"

"It'll be okay. Start backing to the stairs. I think we can get out through the graveyard."

"Quit whispering and drop that mermaid. I've been waiting for years to get my hands on her and you aren't going to stop me."

"How'd you know it was here?"

"I know who hid her. That's all you need to know. Put her back in the trunk and back away. Now!"

Catie gave a startled gasp. "Peter! She's got a knife!"

His flashlight dropped from the woman's face to illuminate five inches of bright sharp steel. It was a switchblade she had pulled out of the depths of her purse. "Give me the mermaid or I will hurt you!" Her arm raised and went into the throw position, her face still and determined. They had no doubt she would do exactly what she claimed.

Peter crouched down in front of the chest as if he was going to do what she demanded. He then saw a scrap of paper he hadn't seen before and snatched it. "Run, Catie! Now!"

As Catie scrambled behind him, the woman gave a frustrated scream. "Stop! I warned you!" Her arm suddenly snapped and the knife sailed across the dark attic.

Prepared for that, Peter had grabbed the ghoul out of the other trunk and thrust it over his head as he stayed down. The knife landed in the middle of the green head and stuck. Peter threw the mannequin down and ran after Catie. Already halfway down the stairs, the terrified girl kept going when she saw Peter start to follow her.

"Head back to the graveyard! Hurry!"

The two burst back through the hidden panel in the ballroom and slid the door shut behind them. With the hope the woman in the attic wouldn't know which way they went, they reentered the graveyard and ran in the opposite direction. Careful not to step on any of the effects or trip over the numerous wires and cables, they looked for one thing: a sign that read Exit.

They saw the welcome red words glowing to their right. As they headed for the way out, they had to squeeze through the row of empty, still Doom Buggies stopped on the track. When they pushed through the door, there was a flight of stairs. Another door blocked their way, but this one led them just where they wanted to be. They were now outside the show building on the other side of the berm.

Their eyes blinked rapidly in the bright sunlight of the waning afternoon as they looked in each direction. "Where do we go, Peter? I…I don't know where we are."

Peter heard the panic in her voice and knew it was up to him to calm his friend. "We're okay, Catie. I know exactly where we are and I know how to get to Dad and Michael. Are you okay to run some more? We have a ways to go."

Catie put a hand on her chest as if that would stop the pounding of her heart. "I can run. I don't want to stop running."

At the pleading look on her face, he pulled her in for a quick hug. He needed one, too. "We'll be all right. Come on. We have to go this way. See the Monorail track over there? Look, there goes Big Red. I know how to get to New Orleans Square from here."

Hand in hand, they ran across the wide backside of the show building. There were cars and trucks parked nearby and they passed another door that led into the Mansion building. The familiar sound of the steam train could be heard as it pulled into the Frontierland Station and they knew they were close to their goal.

Peter's "borrowed" Key to Disneyland once again came in handy to get into the next building. When they came out the other side, it turned out to be the façade of one of the structures behind the train station. With the hope that they wouldn't attract too much attention, they calmly walked across the track behind the parked train and climbed onto the loading platform.

"Dropped my shoe." Peter felt he had to mutter some kind of excuse to a guest who stopped to stare at the two kids who shouldn't have been back there. "'Scuse me."

They slowly walked the length of the platform to the exit ramp right next to the outer edge of the Mansion's queue. "Now, just turn right and go to the Blue Bayou. I think we're in the clear."

As they cut behind Magnolia Park, resplendent in spring blooms, and then behind the French Market, Catie suddenly froze. "Peter! She…she's over there looking for us! On the other side of the tables."

Without even a glance, Peter grabbed Catie's hand and pulled her toward Royal Street and, hopefully, Dad.

Out of the corner of her eye, the woman saw the sudden movement and started to run in the same direction.

"Run, Peter! She saw us!"

They ran as fast as the crowd would let them, dodging aside and muttering, "Sorry," just about every foot of the way. They turned the corner of Royal Street just as their pursuer arrived at the far end, a triumphant smile on her face when she thought she had them blocked. No matter which way they ran, she could head them off so they

ing to get Mom to let him drive the Bird. He's way too tall to fit behind the wheel." After a disbelieving shake of his head, he gave a contented sigh and put his arms behind his wavy brown hair. As he lay back on the deck, the heat felt good as it soaked through his thin shirt. "I didn't go just because I wanted to know what you two have been finding lately. You never told me what you found out about the mermaid."

Catie gave a little gasp and looked quickly toward the house to see if her grandparents were anywhere near. "Alex! Shh! Grandma Margaret and Papa might hear you! We all agreed not to say anything until we knew exactly what it is that we found."

"Nothing yet?"

Peter and Catie just shook their heads. They were frustrated by their lack of progress. There had been no record or pictures of any red-haired mermaid at Disneyland except Ariel—and they were pretty sure she wasn't what they needed. Peter hadn't told anyone else, but he was sure he had been followed through Tomorrowland by that woman from the Haunted Mansion. He had turned quickly to catch her, but she had melted into the shadows and he never saw her again. His gut told him that hadn't been the first—or last—time that had happened.

"Why the long faces? It's too nice a day for that."

The three young faces in question jerked toward the intruding voice. John Michaels chuckled to himself at their expression. His son Adam used to look just like that when he was caught doing something he wasn't supposed to be doing. The twins perfectly mirrored their father. *Life is never boring with kids.* John almost asked what they were up to just to see what they might actually tell him. *Nah, I'll let them off the hook.* "Your grandmother has lunch ready. Come on in. And wipe your feet dry!"

Margaret was setting a pitcher of iced tea on the kitchen table when they all silently trooped into the house. Noticing their serious demeanor, she threw a questioning look at her husband. His shrug told her he knew nothing. "I made a nice tofu salad." That did the trick.

Disgust evident on their faces, they all stared at her in disbelief, each obviously struggling to remain polite.

"Just kidding. We're having pizza."

The rapid recovery of youth took over and the talk during lunch became more animated as the pizza rapidly disappeared.

Between bites, John got a big smile on his face. "Say, did I ever tell you kids about the time I got caught sneaking into Disneyland?"

There was a united, unenthused drone of, "Yes."

"Oh, guess I told you that already."

"Grandma, speaking of Disneyland...."

There was a mumble from John across the table. "I *was* trying to speak about Disneyland...."

Alex continued as if he hadn't heard. "Is it okay if we show Peter the stuff you have stored in the attic? I don't think he's seen some of those ancient things before."

Margaret glanced out of the corner of her eye at John when he tried to cover his laugh with a cough. He knew she didn't like her cherished me-to pieces, Catie hastily put the lid back and moved to the next box marked Memories.

This box held an assortment of ticket stubs to movie theaters and concerts, Disneyland entry tickets, a small gray canister, some jewelry, a large plastic harp of some kind, and a lot of pictures. Catie took out the gold harp and set it aside when she found it didn't actually make any music. After glancing through the movie stubs and not recognizing any of the titles, she turned to the pictures. Assuming the young woman in most of the pictures was her grandmother, she did wonder about all the different men who were in the pictures. "Grandma Margaret was really pretty. And popular." Catie had a smile on her face as she continued to look through the photos, some creased and a few ripped. Her smile froze when she came across one certain picture. Her grandmother was resting alongside a pool with five other girls, all smiling for the camera.

"Peter! Alex! You have to see this! It's Grandma at a pool!"

The boys screwed up their faces. "We really don't want to see a picture of Grandma in a swim suit. I mean, *really* don't want to see that."

"Alex, you have to see this."

At her insistent voice and seeing that she wasn't going to bring it to them, Alex and Peter reluctantly dragged themselves over to her location. After rolling their eyes at seeing the wedding dress, they resigned themselves to whatever they were about to witness. "Okay, but you're probably going to scar us for life. What is it?"

Catie didn't respond to the sarcasm. She pointed at the brunette in the picture. "That's

Grandma!"

Peter's face was the first to register the surprise. "She's a mermaid. Look at the tail. They're all wearing tails! What is this?"

Alex grabbed the photograph from his sister's hand. "Grandma's a mermaid?"

Catie reached behind her and picked up the harp. "One of the other girls is holding this. See? Hey, what does it say on the back of that picture? I see some writing."

Alex turned the photograph over. "1965—Disneyland Hotel." He lowered the picture and looked at Peter and Catie. "There were mermaids at the Hotel? I never heard of that."

"It said 1965. Was there even a Hotel way back then?" Catie didn't know quite as much of Disneyland's history as her friend Peter did and directed her question to him.

Peter just barely heard her. His mind had gone back to the mermaid they had found inside the Haunted Mansion and wondered if there could possibly be a connection. When he realized the twins waited for an answer, he pulled his eyes from the photo. "Yeah, the Disneyland Hotel was there way before that. Do you think we can ask your grandmother about this? If that is her, she might know something that could help us."

Alex looked at all the wedding finery that his sister had pulled out of the chest. "Hey, were you even supposed to be in there? Grandma might not want you poking around in her stuff like that."

The boys were baffled when Catie blushed a bright pink and turned away to put the lovely dress and the other things carefully back in the wooden box. Her voice was so low they almost couldn't hear her. "She knows."

They chose to ignore the girl's embarrassment. "Then, let's go ask. Do you want to bring that gold plastic thing, too?"

Margaret was found relaxing on the back patio as she enjoyed the late afternoon breeze. Her former pique had been replaced by her sense of humor. "So, did you guys find anything interesting in all my ancient things?"

She had a moment of confusion when the plastic harp was thrust in front of her face. The look was quickly replaced by one of happy recognition. "My lyre!"

"Liar?" Alex wasn't sure who she was referring to. "Me? I didn't say anything!"

Margaret gave her grandson a fond smile. "Oh, no, honey. Not liar. Lyre." She spelled out the word and held up the curved plastic. "It's an *ancient*," she stressed with a half smile, "musical instrument. Like a harp. Gosh, haven't seen this in years. What else did you find?"

She took the picture from Catie's hand. "Oh, it's the girls! My, haven't thought about them in so long. That's Betsy and Mary and Omah and…. Hmm, can't remember these other girls' names. Oh, we had so much fun playing the mermaids. Lots of training and that chlorine in the water…. Almost ruined my hair…."

"That really is you."

Margaret pulled back from her memories. She had forgotten the three kids were still standing there staring at her. "I never told you about the mermaids in the Submarine Lagoon? Really? How in the world could I have forgotten that?"

After Peter's warning to Alex in the attic, they really didn't want to say anything about memory loss in old people. They wisely decided to remain quiet and just shrugged their shoulders.

Margaret took their silence as acceptance. "Well, sit down and I'll tell you the story of the Mermaids of Disneyland."

Chapter 2

Flashback — Disneyland — 1959

"Say, Walt, how do you think the re-opening of Tomorrowland went?"

Walt Disney looked up from the small black notebook he had pulled out of his pocket. Protected from the summer sun by a large red and white striped canopy, he sat in a quiet corner of the Carnation Plaza Gardens. All the festivities of the day had tired him and Walt knew he only had a couple of hours before the Disneyland Band was scheduled to perform on the Gardens bandstand. With a slight smile on his face, he swallowed his tired sigh. *Maybe I should have just gone to my apartment.* "Hey, Joe. Well, I think June 14th will be marked as an important date in Disneyland's history, don't you?"

Taking the smile as a good sign, Joe pulled out one of the white wire chairs and sat. After a curious glance at the little black book that Walt quickly put back in his pocket, Joe fanned his face with his hat.

"Yeah, I think so, too. The Matterhorn looks great, the Monorail didn't catch on fire when Mr. Nixon rode it, and none of the mermaids drowned in the Lagoon! Yeah, it was a good day!"

Walt chuckled at the concise description of what was the grand conclusion of an expansion that had cost over seven and a half million dollars and was televised to over ninety million viewers. "I haven't seen her to ask, but did Harriet ever find that mermaid statue that was stolen?"

"No. Pretty lousy timing, too, if you ask me. She was pretty upset no one got to see it before the re-opening."

The boss looked over toward the entrance of Tomorrowland and the prominent House of the Future. Just beyond the unique plastic house was the Avenue of the Flags and a steadily moving mass of guests. He knew there were huge lines at the three new attractions. His new Tomorrowland was already deemed a success. "The live mermaids were a good idea. I heard they were a big hit in the parade down Main Street, too."

Joe nodded. He had worried that it would turn into an ugly shoving match when the girls began to toss strands of pearls from the treasure chest on their float. But, everyone behaved themselves. "Half the girls were on the float with King Triton and the other half were in the Lagoon, as you saw. The ballet went well?"

Walt looked confused for a moment. "Ballet? Oh, you mean the swimming the girls were doing. Yeah, they did well. I pulled a couple of them aside before they got all wet to have their picture taken with Nixon. One of them had no idea who he was!"

When Joe complained about the June heat,

Walt sent him back to Tomorrowland to get a couple of drinks from the Yacht Bar. With a secret smile, Walt knew he probably had just bought himself another hour before Joe would make it back. That part of the Park was packed.

His reprieve, however, was short-lived. One of the security guards silently appeared next to Walt's chair. Feeling the man's presence rather than actually hearing him, Walt glanced up at the dark face beside him. "Hello, Wolf. Thought I'd see you today. Have a seat."

Wolf's sharp blue eyes continued to scan the Park as he declined the offer with a shake of his head. "Just wanted to see if you needed anything. You all right?"

"Just a little tired, but, then, we all are."

Wolf nodded his agreement and remained characteristically quiet.

Walt wanted to see if he could push one of Wolf's few buttons. "So, tell me. What do you think of the new mermaids?"

A small smile came and went over Wolf's handsome face. "I think you made a good decision to include them in the Lagoon."

Walt gave a chuckle. "That's not what I meant."

"I know."

His boss's head slowly shook side to side. "You're one of a kind, Wolf. Have a seat. I'd like you to tell me about the girls' tryouts over at the Disneyland Hotel. I've heard various renditions and I'd like to hear yours."

Wolf knew it wasn't a request and reluctantly sat on the red and white striped seat. "How did you know I was there?"

Walt just gave him a wide smile.

"Well, you knew that over three hundred girls showed up after that newspaper ad came out."

At Walt's brief nod, Wolf continued. "They were all lined up in rows and, if they were tapped on the shoulder, they were dismissed. It took a couple of hours for the number to get down to fifty." Wolf gave another smile. "Yes, they were all very pretty, all of them had long hair, and none were over twenty-five years old. One of the girls did have a fake ponytail that came off when it was tugged. She didn't even wait for the tap on her shoulder and left in tears."

"Then what happened?"

"The instructors made sure all of them could swim and then tied their arms together above their heads. Another soft cloth was used to bind their legs at the knees and ankles. They were dropped in the water at the deep end and had to make it to the shallow end, swimming like a dolphin. A few of them panicked and had to be helped out of the water." At Walt's pointed look, he added, "No, I wasn't one of the rescuers. One of the girls who made it to the finals actually sank like a rock at first and scraped her stomach on the bottom of the pool. I think the instructors were impressed by her determination and how long she could hold her breath."

"So, the final eight were chosen out of the bunch that made it to the shallow end alive."

"Yeah, something like that. They were pretty excited to hear they would be making $45 a week and only two girls would work at a time in one hour shifts during the day."

Walt nodded. "Well, the minimum wage is one dollar an hour. I didn't feel that was right considering how hard they would have to train in water ballet and synchronized swimming for weeks before the Lagoon opened."

"They didn't bat an eye when they found out the water in the Lagoon was only fifty degrees. They were all just happy to have been selected."

Walt gave a snort. "Do you know how expensive it would be to heat that Lagoon? It has nine million gallons of water! I figured that large flat rock out in the middle would get warm enough from the sun and then there's the heat from the submarines, too. That rubber fin weighs, what, three pounds? That should help keep their legs warm."

"Well, I'm assigned to be there when their first shift is over. To make sure they all get backstage all right." He paused, but didn't receive the crack he had expected to hear. "I'll see how they're doing and report back if there are any problems."

The anticipated broad smile now broke out on Walt's face. "Oh, I'm sure you will. How many fellas did you have to beat out to get that privilege?"

Wolf didn't take the bait. He stood from his chair and gave his boss and friend a look completely devoid of expression. "Eight. Anything else you need, Walt?"

"No, I'm good, Wolf. Thanks! Joe'll be back soon with a couple of drinks. See you around." After Wolf melted back into the shadows of the Castle, Walt was still chuckling as he pulled the notebook out of his pocket and wrote Mermaids on the top of a blank page.

Yorba Linda

"So, when I saw the ad in the paper in 1965 that said Disneyland was bringing back the mermaids for the Park's tenth anniversary, I just had to try out."

Catie was all ears as Margaret continued her story. They had moved to the attic so Margaret could get the other photographs. Catie had dozens of questions in mind. "Were there very many girls? I would have loved to have tried out for that."

Alex gave an amused snort and couldn't resist a brotherly chide. "You barely know how to swim! You'd sink right to the bottom. I bet I could do it better than you!"

"Yeah, Alex, I think you'd make a much prettier mermaid than Catie would!"

Alex turned red at Peter's comment. He hadn't meant it to come out that way. "Hey! That's not...."

Margaret knew she had better step into the fray before it got out of hand. "All right, you three. Knock it off! Alex, quit teasing your sister. Peter, quit being your dad. Catie...."

"Hey, what did I do!?"

"I was just going to answer your question, dear." *That car show is sounding better and better by the moment.* "There were almost one hundred girls who showed up for the audition, but I didn't know any of them. Gosh, I was only eighteen." Margaret gave a wistful sigh for all the years that had gone by. It seemed so long ago. "We had our legs and arms tied together and had to swim from one end of the Disneyland Hotel pool to the other. Now, it was a completely different pool than it is today. None of the fancy decorations and slides. Just a huge plain rectangle. "

"How'd you do, Grandma?" Alex figured he had better join in the conversation and deflect what had just happened.

"Sank like a rock and died."

"Really?"

"No." She laughed at the looks on their faces. She loved testing to see how far their politeness and manners would stretch. "I did pretty well. There were only six of us who were picked." She again held up the photo to look at the faces. "We all became pretty good friends and stayed in touch even after they stopped having the mermaids in the Lagoon. This girl," she pointed at a pretty brunette, "was one of my bridesmaids."

"Why did they stop? It sounded like the guests in the Park really enjoyed them."

"Oh, they did." Margaret's eyes sparkled at one particular memory. "Some of the gentlemen guests got a little over-enthused and actually jumped into the Lagoon to come see us. We were so far away from the edge of the Lagoon and with all the noise from the subs, we couldn't hear what anyone shouted. So, we just had to wave and smile at everyone. Those guys apparently took it as an invitation. I wasn't there that day, but I sure heard a lot about it. But, it was all the chlorine in the water that finally got to us. My hair is brown, so it didn't happen to me, but one of the girls had blonde hair and it turned green. It was hard on our skin, too."

"How did you get into the Lagoon, Grandma?"

Margaret had picked up the plastic harp and held it in her arms as she would have done years ago. "Hmmm? Oh, there was a special tube cham-

ber. You see, we were supposed to just mysteri-
ously appear in the Lagoon. It would have ruined
the effect if the guests had seen our helper dump us
into the water. We couldn't very well walk in those
heavy fins. Sometimes the guys helping us would
be in a bad mood and would just drop us whether
we were ready or not. I wish your grandfather had
been working in that part of the Park then to be a
helper and not that other guy."

"Papa worked at the Haunted Mansion, didn't
he?"

"That's right, Alex. He started there in 1962,
but I hadn't met him yet. Then he worked on the
new tower of the Disneyland Hotel in 1965. He and
all his construction friends had quite a time watching us girls learning our movements for the synchronized swimming."

"How did you meet him, Grandma?"

Margaret recognized the starry-eyed look on
Catie's face. "Oh, he managed to have one of his
friends push him into the pool while we were prac-
ticing. Landed right on top of me. Just like he had
planned it, I found out later. The construction guys
had made up some lame excuse to be near the pool
instead of working on the Tower like they should
have been doing. Something about making sure
the pool hadn't been cracked by all the jackhammer
use in the area. Something stupid like that."

"Was it love at first sight?"

"Well, considering he almost knocked me out,
no! But, those big blue eyes of his and that wavy
blonde hair did more to get me to forgive him than
his apologies."

The boys were already tired of the mushy stuff
and wanted to get back to the Lagoon. "Grandma,

what was that thing used for?"

With a small smile, Margaret allowed the boys to distract her. She knew Catie would be back privately for more information. "My lyre? That was just a prop we used in the Lagoon. Some of the girls had huge plastic combs for their hair, and some had shell-shaped mirrors. We had to swim down when the submarines went by and wave at the passengers inside or do some synchronized swimming. Sometimes for fun we would dive down and re-arrange the fish that floated in the water!" She could see the boys were more interested in hearing about the pranks. "I remember one time in particular." Margaret looked away and grinned to herself. "Gosh, I haven't thought about this in years. Once I met your grandfather, everything changed."

Peter let a groan escape his lips. He gave her a sheepish look when her eyebrows rose. "Sorry."

"What I was going to say, Peter, is that I found something weird underwater. One day two of us were in the water and I was on the port side of the sub as it went by. After I went to the surface to get a breath, I dove again and tried to move one of the larger grouper fish. It was tied down pretty securely, but I saw something wedged under the coral rock next to the fish. I dug it out it and went back up before the next sub came by. Since it wasn't a prop that we were supposed to use, I had to stash it out of sight behind our rock. The other girls had no idea what it might be, so I called dibs and put it under my wrap when we left the Lagoon that evening."

"What was it, Grandma?"

Margaret didn't answer as she reached over into the Memory box Catie had discovered. She pulled out one of the objects and held it up for them to see.

"What is it?" Alex held out his hand for it and lightly shook it. He couldn't hear anything inside. "Did you open it? What's was in it?"

With a shrug, Margaret shook her head. "You know, it was so long ago I can't even remember. I must have opened it at some point. I think…."

As Catie was handed the object, Peter was silent. He could only stare at it, his mouth slightly open in the surprise that overwhelmed him. He knew exactly what it was.

It was a gray capsule just like the ones he had found at Disneyland with his brother Michael. It had to contain a long-forgotten clue from Walt Disney. And it was right there in front of him.

CHAPTER 3

Flashback — Disneyland — 1965

"We hope the undersea voyage you are about to take will encourage your interest in the wonderful life in the sea."

"Did you hear that, Ken? It definitely said we were going under the sea."

Ken, Anne and their daughter Ruth inched through the crowded queue as they got closer to the large gray submarines. The *Seawolf* had just sedately sailed past in the colorful lagoon on their left, its hull still wet and dripping from the waterfalls.

"I think I see a fish!"

Ken settled Ruth more comfortably on his shoulders as she squirmed about. The submarine was closely watched until it disappeared under the waterfall at the far end of the lagoon. "I think all the fish are underwater, sweetie."

"I *really* don't want to get my hair wet, Ken. We've talked about this already." Anne's hand went up to touch her elaborate hairdo. After hours in the

rently enroute to the polar ice-cap and will then probe depths seldom seen by man."

A bed of bright green kelp lightly brushed against the windows as the submarine continued its voyage. A school of silver fish could be seen circling in the distance as huge lobsters shook their claws at the passengers who stared at them.

"As they roam the bottom of the coastal seas, giant groupers are always in search of food. Speaking of giants, that giant clam has a fluted shell that can weigh up to a quarter of a ton. That moray eel has powerful tooth-filled jaws and likes to ambush unwary prey from holes in the beautiful reef."

"Mommy, look! That snake thing tried to attack us! Hey, those red fish are fighting with each other!"

"Those are lobsters…which I would rather be having for dinner right about now than watching out that thin, tiny window…. Oh, no, now what?" Anne's clammy hand touched her throat as a warning bell was sounded.

"Weather alert! All controls… take her down eight degrees. Hold her at eight fathoms and proceed on course."

Anne's arms went over her head in an unneeded effort to protect her hair as the thunderous sound of water pounded on the hull. Her porthole was obscured by a torrent of water as the ship passed under the first waterfall.

"Sharks! I see sharks!"

Just like Ruth, an enthralled Ken pressed his face closer to his porthole as everything became dimmer the further they got from the sunlight.

"Submarines can dive safely below the violent surface of the ocean during storms. Other craft have not been so fortunate. Here you witness their fate. The graveyard of lost ships—and a stronghold of sunken treasure!"

The beautiful coral and plant life grew up and around the remnants of the sunken wooden ships from many different cultures and eras. Sharks guarded their secrets as they silently circled the wrecks. Two deep sea divers were struggling to lift an encrusted, heavy treasure chest while an octopus waved its tentacles at them.

"We've raised the Polar ice-cap, sir! The ice is thickening."

"Take her down. Ladies and gentlemen, we are now passing under the North Pole into a place where the sun has never penetrated. This is the realm of eternal darkness and the creatures here have their own eerie luminescence."

"I can't see anything, Daddy."

"That's the point, honey. Just keep looking, Ruthie."

A small shriek was heard as a strange fish with long teeth and a light dangling from its forehead suddenly appeared and vanished just as quickly.

"Captain! Giant squid ahead!"

"Stand by with the repellant charge. Steady.....The legends tell us that ships are crushed by the powerful tentacles of a giant squid. But, these are just legends told by ancient mariners and have no basis in fact. They should be classified as fiction along with the other tales of...mermaids? I don't believe it, Mate. Check the air pressure in the cabin!"

The huge squid struggling with a captured black and white whale vanished from their view and a sunken treasure trove was seen with its beautiful inhabitants.

"Mermaids! Look, Daddy! Look, that red-haired one is trying on a crown!"

The mermaids too quickly vanished from their view as the scenery changed to one of destruction. Stone columns and huge statues were seemingly strewn about on the ocean floor.

"These crumbling heaps betray the hand of man. These classic ruins could very well be the legendary lost city of Atlantis believed to have been destroyed by a tremendous volcano."

"Ken? What's that rumbling noise?" Anne pulled her face from the viewing port and tried to see her husband in the dim light of the interior.

Red lights and erupting clouds of bubbles suddenly came from the shifting ruins and the submarine shook side to side.

"Helmsman, steer clear of the tottering ruins! We now appear to be safe from the volcanic activity…."

The Captain was interrupted by the mate. "Sir? The sonar reports an unidentifiable condition dead ahead. Uhm, sir? It…it looks like a sea serpent!"

All faces in the submarine pressed closer to their windows at the long, sinewy, scaled body that seemed to go on forever. There was a brief laugh from the guests as they came face-to-face with the silly face and rolling eyes of the 'monster.'

"You're right, Mate, it is a sea serpent! No, don't enter it in the log. Nobody would believe it. I think we have been submerged too long. Stand by to surface!"

"Thank goodness." Anne's mumble could be heard by those seated around her. Ken gave a chuckle as the submarine gave three blasts on its horn and the exit waterfall could be heard thundering on the hull.

Once docked and given the 'all clear,' the guests retraced their steps and climbed the circular staircase. With a sigh of relief, Anne lifted her face to the welcome sun and took a breath of fresh air.

"So, what did you think, honey?" Ken tried to mask his enthusiasm. He was ready to go get in line again.

"I loved it!"

Anne gave their daughter a fond, but disbelieving, look before she answered. "Well, you were right, Ken. My hair is safe. But, whoever heard of a red-headed mermaid?"

As the family walked off to get in line for the Matterhorn bobsleds, Ken just bided his time until he could ride the submarines again.

Yorba Linda

"**C**an we open it, Grandma?"

"I don't see why not." Margaret looked at the eager faces that surrounded her and her glance rested on Peter. He seemed a little too pale and too quiet compared to her grandkids. "You okay, Peter?"

His wide green eyes jerked up from the canister that was still in Catie's hands. After a swallow, a fake grin was plastered on his face in an attempt to hide what he felt must be a guilty expression. "Yeah, I'm great! Uh huh. Just excited, that's all." *Quit talking. You sound stupid.*

"All right." Margaret's words were slow as she

tried to analyze his odd reaction. Since his father
Lance had been best friends with her boy Adam
ever since college, she had known Peter practically
since birth. Lance was like another son to her and
she knew Peter had the same quirks and qualities
as his charming father. There was something that
just wasn't right, but she wasn't sure how to find out
what it was. "Do you want to do the honors, Peter?"
The gray capsule was taken from the disappointed
Catie and held out to their friend.

As he eagerly reached for the item under discussion, he noticed the hurt looks on both Catie's
and Alex's faces. "No, that's okay. Alex or Catie
should open it." When his hands dropped to his
sides, his fingers were clenched in a tight fist.

Without a word from his grandmother, Alex
grabbed the canister. "I'll do it! Hey, this is really
tight."

"You need to work it loose with something else
first." Three faces turned to Peter at his mumbled
comment. Eyes wide again, he hastily added,
"Umm, at least, I think you should try something like
that."

After a 'what's wrong with you?' look at Peter,
Catie turned back to the Memory box. She had
spotted something in there that might help. "Will
this work?"

Margaret bit back a groan as Alex took the col-
lectible gold bottle opener from the early 1960's.
The plastic domed center of the opener protected a
golden Sleeping Beauty Castle and a waving
Mickey Mouse. Without a glance at the ornate
golden filigree, Alex dug at the gray plastic cap.
*Maybe he won't bend it all up.... Okay, maybe John
can bend it back into shape....*

"I think it's loose!" Alex tossed aside the battered tool and tried his hardest to turn the stubborn end cap. "Wait, there it goes!" As the cap turned off its threaded home of over fifty years, all the occupants of the attic eagerly leaned forward to see what was hidden inside. Alex looked disappointed when only a small gold key and a piece of paper fell out of the upended canister. "That's all?" He held up the key and looked at it. "What good is that? What does it go to?"

Peter's voice was almost a whisper. "Maybe you need to read what it says on the…the paper." He had almost called it a page out of Walt's diary.

Margaret threw another quick glance at Peter. He had become more and more strained. With a quick snag of the paper before one of the kids could get it, she read it through one time to herself. A look of recognition came across her face and she broke out into a broad smile. "Oh, now I remember this! I did open it. Now I remember. It was just as hard to get open the first time, too. Almost gave up…. Here, listen to this. I don't know who wrote it, but it says:

"Past the redhead in Atlantis you sail.
Use this key to unlock the Mermaid's Tale."

At the words redhead and mermaid, Catie and Peter shot a look at each other and gave a quick shake of their heads. They would hold onto their secret for a while longer until they found out what Margaret knew.

The note was passed around as Margaret took the key from Alex. "At the time I thought I knew what this poem meant. You guys never saw it, but the original Submarine Voyage had mermaids way knew it was one from the attic. "What did you find? Something about the mermaid?"

With a shaky finger Catie pointed at the woman on the far right. Dressed in their mermaid tails, the four girls were relaxing alongside the pool at the Disneyland Hotel. "Is that who I think it is?"

Peter peered closer at the picture. His mouth opened to say something but just clamped shut again. It was unbelievable if it was true. "Is that her mother?" His eyes darted up to Catie's pale face.

"I don't think that's her mother. I think that's the woman who attacked us in the Haunted Mansion. That's her, Peter!"

"It can't be, Catie. Look how long it's been since that was taken. Look how old....well, you know what I mean....look at your grandma. She kinda looks like this photo, but she was young here. It just can't be her," he repeated even though his mind told him Catie was right. She looked just like the woman from the Haunted Mansion. For the first time Peter wished his parents would hurry up and get there to take him home. He wanted some time to himself to sort through all this. "Your grandma agreed to let me take the key and the note from you-know-who. Maybe she can tell us this girl's name and let me have the picture."

"She's used to me asking her all kinds of questions. I'll ask her and get the photograph for you. Do you think this has something to do with our mermaid?"

Peter's head moved up and down like a bobblehead doll. "Yeah, I do. And I'm going to try and get some answers before Wednesday."

Catie looked confused. "Why Wednesday? What's so important about Wednesday?"

"That's when your family leaves for Marceline, Missouri, and Toonfest."

"Oh, I forgot about that. I wish you were going with us."

"Yeah, me, too, but I think I can get more accomplished here."

They became silent as they contemplated the probable link between this new clue and the mermaid they had already found. What bothered both of them was the mysterious woman who had accosted them in the Mansion. How was she involved with all this and how could she possibly be the woman in the photograph that was dated over fifty years ago?

Peter knew that their next encounter with the redheaded woman would not be pleasant.

that was to come and talk to them before he jumped into anything. Then there was always Wolf.

Wolf had helped Catie and him before. Wolf had been around forever—a term that carried a lot more meaning now that he had traveled with Wolf and discovered his secret. Wolf knew Disneyland inside out and backward, a lot better than he did.

Peter turned to look out his bedroom window, but his gaze was unseeing. Did he really want to ask Wolf for help? Was that woman from the Mansion still out there somewhere? He had already seen her once. How many times had she been there when he *hadn't* seen her? With a startled jerk of his head, Peter's gaze now became focused. *She might be right outside watching the house*. As he stood from his chair, Peter went to the side of the window, just out of sight, and let his eyes move slowly across their huge backyard. His thoughts moved to the thief, Todd Raven, and how he had infiltrated their house during a party just a few months ago. Kimberly, his mom, had been tied up and Todd had tried to take him captive. It was Wolf who came to his rescue.

Not seeing any movement in the yard other than their Golden retriever puppy, Dug, living up to her name, Peter made the decision that he should talk to Wolf. The only information he had been able to find on the Internet about any Submarine Voyage artifacts was a 2005 auction that had been held at the Disneyland Resort. The article mentioned a sea serpent like the one Margaret had mentioned, along with a shark fighting an octopus and two fighting lobsters that had been auctioned off. That brief article mentioned something else, though. It seems a "redhead" was supposed to be included in the sale, but had disappeared beforehand. Peter wondered if the redhead in the article could possibly be the mermaid he now had on his desk. *Only one way to find out.* After a quick glance at his wall clock, Peter realized his dad would leave for his job at Disneyland in just a minute and he had better hurry so he could go along and find Wolf.

"Isn't this a school night?" Wolf bit back a smile when Peter tried to hide the fact that he just rolled his eyes.

"You sound like my mom."

"Your mom wouldn't let you be here if it was a school night."

"True. But we have the week off for some parent-teacher thing. Dad has the night-shift so he let me come with him. He just told me to be at the Hungry Bear right before closing time."

Wolf could see Peter's eyes continually dart around as he talked. He seemed disconcerted for some reason, uneasy. "Something wrong or are you just trying to pick up girls?"

"Ewww."

That worked. Peter broke out of his on-edge stance and turned to stare unbelievingly at his friend. Before Peter could get defensive, Wolf stopped him. "You have something you want to tell me."

"How'd you know?"

Wolf gave a rare smile. "I've known you since birth. And I've known your dad even longer. You're just like him."

"So everybody says...."

"You don't need to mumble. That's not *neces-*

sarily a bad thing. Walk with me while I patrol Fantasyland."

"Oh, yeah. I forgot you're on duty."

"Peter. I'm in my Security uniform...."

"Wait a sec." Wolf turned back to see Peter pull off his ever-present backpack. A search through every pocket started slowly but became more frantic the longer it continued. Peter finally heaved a sigh of relief. "Here it is. Thought I put it in the zipper pouch." A small piece of yellowed paper was handed to Wolf. He nodded when he saw Wolf's eyes widen. "Yeah, I figured you'd recognize the handwriting."

"It's from Walt. Where did you get this?"

"Can we walk while I tell you?" Night hadn't completely fallen as their steps turned toward the Castle now ablaze in a myriad of colored lights. His voice betrayed his excitement and frustration as Peter proceeded to tell the tale. Beginning with his discovery in the Mansion's attic, he went up to the point Margaret let Alex open the gray canister. As he described the encounter with the strange woman, he could sense the tension build in Wolf.

"She threw a knife at you? And you didn't tell anyone!?"

"Well, she did miss."

Wolf's words were punctuated with the anger he felt inside. "That. Is. Not. The. Point. And. You. Know. It."

When he saw the look on Wolf's face, Peter knew not to push it. Wolf looked like he was ready to punch something. "I'm sorry. I guess I should have. But...."

"But what?" Hands on his hips, Wolf had stopped in front of Mr. Toad's Wild Ride and turned to face the boy.

"But I wanted to try and solve this mystery my-self. Well, with Catie, too, of course. You know how exciting it is to have something like this to solve."

Wolf had to remind himself he was talking with a twelve-year-old and not the boy's adult father. He put a hand on Peter's head in an understanding gesture and his voice softened. "Yeah, I know." The warm, fuzzy moment didn't last long. "And I'm not even going to start on the fact that you should-n't have been inside the Mansion in the first place." There was a moment of tense silence as he stared at Peter's face. He could tell the boy vacillated be-tween being worried about getting in trouble and re-lieved that he had someone to talk to. With a shake of his head, Wolf drew in a calming breath. "Now, tell me about that woman again. What did she look like?"

"I don't know!" Peter threw up his hands in an exasperated gesture. *How do you describe some-one?* Thinking he hit on something, Peter pointed at Wolf. "She was old like you and Dad. I guess I should've brought the picture from Catie's grandma. She kinda looked just the same."

"You'll have to show me tomorrow. I want to see that mermaid, too."

Peter became a little confused as he studied the odd look on Wolf's face. He didn't see the firm determination Wolf usually had at times like this. A slow realization came over him. "You don't know anything about this note or where it leads, do you?" *Rats. That would have solved a lot of problems.*

Wolf again looked at the paper he still held. "No. Walt never told me about any mermaid. I...I don't know why he didn't." A frown came to Wolf's face as he thought about his much-loved and missed boss. Apparently there were still some secrets out there—and it bothered him a lot that he didn't know anything about this particular secret. *Why didn't Walt tell me about this set of clues? And who is this woman who apparently does know about it?* "I might not have been around when he set this into place. Maybe your grandfather knew. It might be in his notes in the War Room somewhere."

"I thought you were always around."

Peter earned a brief smile at that as Wolf motioned for them to get moving again. "I tried to be, but, as you know, it was necessary for me to be gone for a few years. We didn't want people to realize that I didn't age."

"Where'd you go?"

"Hmmm?" Wolf had been deep in thought about the course of events that had led him to where he was at that time. "Oh, here and there. Spent a lot of time with my family."

"Bet the Shaman liked that."

Wolf just nodded as they turned the corner around the Mad Tea Party. The cast members were busy with the last of the blockades from the parade that had just gone by. Peter picked up one of the pale green streamers that had been shot out of a cannon on one of the floats. The remainder of the streamers and confetti were being sucked up by an overgrown-version of a vacuum cleaner. Always on duty, Wolf's attention was drawn to two teenage boys running toward the Bobsled line. "Walk!" They angrily turned and apparently what they were about to shout back died on their lips when they saw it was a security guard telling them—loudly—to slow down. Once the boys got into line, Wolf gave a tilt of his head to Peter. "Let's go down by Small World."

"Just as long as we don't have to...."

"Don't have to what? Peter?" Wolf turned back as the boy had become uncharacteristically quiet. "What's wrong?" He did a quick scan of the moving crowd but could see nothing amiss.

Peter swiveled on his heels and took Wolf's arm. "Just keep moving. Act natural."

"I'd be more natural if you let go of my hand. What's wrong?"

"I think I just saw her! Don't look back! I saw her by Alice. She's watching me."

"Peter. Calm down. Do you mean the woman from the Mansion?" At the boy's nervous nod, Wolf's instincts took over and he began to give commands. "Just walk by my side. I'll handle it. I want you to drop something and look back. Is she still there? What's she wearing?" Wolf kept his voice low and calm and tried to get Peter to settle. The boy looked ready to break and run.

Peter's head jerked side to side and he grabbed the first thing he saw.

"Not my radio! Oh, shoot."

The two-way Security radio made a fizzling sound as it hit the pavement and bounced a couple of feet away. Peter made a show of throwing up his arms. "Oh, I dropped it! I'll get it for you, Wolf."

"Smooth, Peter." The words dripped with unheard sarcasm as Peter wasn't listening to a word he said.

"Yeah, she's still there." The radio was waved about as Peter excitedly turned back to Wolf. "She's wearing a blue shirt and...and, oh, it has

so his concentration turned to the woman who was probably now crouched at the far end of the dock. Still, there were the three Monorail pillars to watch. She could be hidden behind any one of them and try to escape by circling behind him. Wolf let go of his anger and let his senses take over. With his special abilities came exceptional hearing and an acute sense of smell. She wouldn't get around behind him.

With a steady, unhurried walk, Wolf advanced down the dock toward the storage area. There was a light blue railing along the length of the wide walkway that prevented anyone from falling into the water. It would also make it more difficult for the woman to escape to the far banks. Unless she had wings or decided to swim for it, he knew he had her cornered.

As he blocked out the noise of the crowds around them and the screams from the nearby Matterhorn bobsled riders, Wolf could hear nothing else. There was no labored breathing of someone in hiding. There was no scent of fear from someone about to be caught. There was…nothing.

With only one opening into the storage area, Wolf narrowed his eyes and took the last four steps to the entry. "You have no way out. Put your hands where I can see them and come out." He kept his voice low and calm. He waited for a sound from within, some indication that she would comply without a struggle.

There was nothing. No sound. No smell. "Last chance."

When he received no reply, Wolf took a deep breath and stepped into the entryway. His eyes instantly adjusted to the lower light level as he scanned the remnants of ride floats and food carts.

It was empty.

Not believing what he was, or, more specifically, what he was not seeing, he stepped inside. All the various boxes and banners were pushed aside—all the time knowing a person couldn't possibly be hidden behind them.

Confused, he retraced his steps to Peter and took the same care he had taken going in.

When Wolf came back empty-handed, a surprised Peter rose from the bench where he had sat to eat his popcorn. Remnants of kernels fell in a shower from his lap. The birds and ducks would have fun. "What happened? Where is she?"

Wolf's eyes kept moving. "She didn't come back this way? You didn't see her? You sure you weren't distracted?"

Peter just shook his head, a kernel of popcorn stopped halfway to his mouth. "How could she get away? There's no exit, is there? Is there something underground?"

"No, nothing underground there. I don't understand. Are you sure you were paying attention?" Wolf just couldn't believe she had somehow gotten away.

"Hey, I didn't see her again! Are you sure she wasn't hiding?" At Wolf's exasperated look, he shrugged. "Just a suggestion. You want to go look again?" Not knowing what else to do, Peter held out the box of popcorn.

"No, thanks. I need to think about this. I want to compare the face we just saw to your picture. Let's get you back to your dad."

Peter was about to protest that he had another couple of hours before Lance was off duty, but he knew better than to say anything right then. "'Kay."

Wolf found another security guard and used his radio to get Lance's location. Deep in thought and silent, he and Peter headed for Frontierland.

Marceline, Missouri

Catie was happy to get a text from Peter. After three days on the road she was happy for any diversion. They just had a few miles to go before they were at Walt Disney's hometown. She was somewhat confused and worried by the message.

Same woman followed me at DL. Wolf chased her. Lost her at old boat dock. Will let you know if anything new happens.

Alex read the message over her shoulder. Usually she would tell him he had invaded her space and to back off. "What does Peter mean by old boat dock? What old dock? The Mark Twain or the Jungle Cruise? Aren't they boat docks?"

In the front seat, also glad of something new to talk about, their Mom and Dad overheard. "What was that, honey?" Beth turned to face her twins. With a momentary frown, she wondered why they looked so…guilty as their heads shot up in unison. When Catie turned red, Beth figured that was the weak link. "Did you say something about a boat dock? Is that from Peter?"

The twins looked at each other and had a moment of silent discussion. Not always able to finish each other's sentences, they still had a good idea what the other was thinking. With a slight nod, Alex gave his permission for her to talk. "Yeah, it's from

Peter. He said something about an old boat dock, but we aren't sure what he means."

"Do you want some help in figuring it out?" Adam gave a smile. "Your mom and I know a thing or two about boat docks." His smile widened when Beth gave him a playful punch on the arm. He had met Beth on a boat dock many years earlier. "There's the old Keelboat dock, for one."

"Oh, and the Phantom Boats were there for a short time. How about the Motor Boat Cruise? Does Small World count as a boat dock?" Beth was warming up to the game.

"And don't forget Pirates. That would also count." There was silence from the back seat. Adam checked his rear-view mirror and saw the two heads close together. "Kids?"

"Yeah, thanks, Dad." Alex looked at Catie's phone again and whispered to his sister, "Why don't you just text him back and ask."

"There's our turn-off! The GPS says we only have about three miles to go!" Adam swung the Jeep off the I-35 and headed through the slightly rolling hills of farmland. "I'm excited to be back. It seems ages ago that Lance and I were here." He slowed down about halfway to their destination. "Hey, kids, look. That's the farm where Walt lived. We'll come back after we check into the hotel. That's the Dreaming Tree and the old barn is in the back."

Beth put a fond hand on his arm. She knew what Lance and Adam had gone through in their first Hidden Mickey quest. This had been the place that started it all. "I was glad we were able to get into the Uptown Theatre. Thought it would be filled with the animators and cartoonists."

time. "We're on vacation, Dad!"

"Come on. It's only a few blocks away. I want you to see the artwork throughout the school. Back in 1960 when this school was just built, Walt sent his animators out from California to decorate the building. Some of the murals are pretty cool. And, there's a lot of Disney memorabilia, including Walt's desk that has his initials engraved into it."

As Beth and the kids walked over to the gymnasium to see the artwork that encircled the room, Adam slowly wandered through the main hallway to look at all the pictures again. Lost in thought about the first quest that had brought him to this exact spot, he became aware that someone else was by his side. As he turned, the welcoming smile on his face faded. It wasn't Beth.

The tall young woman had her arms folded across her chest as she watched him. There was amusement in her soft brown eyes. About to say something, she took a moment to flip her bangs out of her eyes. When she saw a flicker of recognition at the gesture, she gave a light laugh. "So, it must be refreshing to just walk in here and not have to break in in the middle of the night. Did you learn how to drive yet?"

"Mandy! Is it really you? How long has it been since you stole your mother's keys and let us in?"

She made a show of putting her finger to her lips and shushing him. "Shh. Nobody knows I still do that."

"So, you were what? Three or four when we opened the secret combination? You still playing with the Snow White doll we found?"

"I was eleven, and you know it! And, yes, I still have the doll you gave me."

Adam leaned against the wall as he studied her. "So, the first recipient of our scholarship is all grown up now. What are you up to? Besides breaking into elementary schools."

"Actually I'm still in school. For some reason they asked me to present you with the award tomorrow." She and Adam had hit it off when they first met back in 2002. Lance had been the center of attention and Adam had walked off to the side to do some quiet exploring—much like he had done now. Clearly not enthralled with the handsome Lance, Mandy had struck up a conversation with Adam and had even helped them solve the clue. In the end, after the hunt was over, it seemed right to present Mandy with the first scholarship. "I'm going to come back here to teach art when I get my degree."

"Mandy, that's wonderful!"

"So, where's that other guy?"

"Wow, after all this time you still don't like Lance! That will truly puncture his ego."

She gave a dismissing wave of her hand. "Oh, he has enough to go around."

Adam tilted back his head and gave a laugh. "I can't wait to tell him I saw you again!" He looked over when the door opened and his family came back inside. "Hey, Beth, this is Mandy. You know, the girl who helped Lance and me and got the first scholarship."

"It's really nice to meet you all, but I need to get going. I saw Adam and just couldn't help teasing him again. See you tomorrow at the ceremony."

Mandy waved as she left the building. Adam was smiling as he showed his family the treasures in the hallway.

"**D**ad, are you sure this is the right tree? It doesn't look very good."

The cottonwood tree in discussion was a sorry sight. It had been struck by lightning in 2007, plus the ravages of time and disease had not helped matters. The community had planted a new tree nearby.

"Yeah, that's it, poor thing." Adam had been searching all over the trunk while his family amused themselves reading the signs that had been posted highlighting the special features of Walt's old homestead. "Hey! Here it is! Come here, you guys." Adam was excited as he pointed out a faint impression in the gnarled bark.

"What does it say? I can't tell, Dad."

"Alex, that's Walt's initials. W. E. D. That was what Uncle Lance and I were looking for and showed us where to dig. Yeah, this started it all for us."

"Can we go to the barn? The sign says we can write a message there."

"I want to send Peter a picture of the tree. I'm going with Alex."

"And off they go." Adam shook his head. "After what Peter and Catie went through at Disneyland, I thought they might be more interested in what I had gone through."

Beth took his hand and they slowly walked toward the barn. It was a replica of the barn that had been on the farm in Walt's time, but it was just as emotional an experience for the multitudes who visited. Adam wanted to see if his message was still visible. "Oh, they're young and involved in their own things. How often did you listen to your dad talk about Disneyland and when he worked there?"

Adam had to admit she was right. "Yeah, I guess you're right. At least now you've seen the first part of the quest. You didn't come in until later."

Beth looked around at the lovely scenery by the small lake and gave his arm a squeeze. "I'm very happy to be here! I was hoping you would say yes when Toonfest asked you to come. We'd better go see what the twins are doing. I don't want them fighting over some choice spot to write their names.... What are you doing?"

Adam had walked around the side of the barn, past the rail fence that marked the entrance. "Just wanted to look a little more closely, that's all."

Beth gave a knowing smile. "Looking for another clue?" Her smile faded as she thought about it. "Do you think there might be another one here? This isn't the same barn, you know." In spite of her words, her eyes began to scan the upright slats that made up the side.

"Yeah, I know." Adam gave a self-conscious laugh. "I guess I'm just caught up in the memories. There couldn't possibly be something else here."

"You're probably right. We're just being silly."

But, as they neared the entrance, their eyes were continually moving.

CHAPTER 5

Flashback — Disneyland — 1965

"**W**ell, what do you have to report? It's been a while since I've heard from you." Walt looked up from the papers on the table next to his tapestry-covered wingback chair. A frown crossed his face as his visitor turned back from the window that over-looked Main Street. He had come to his apartment to get some uninterrupted work done—and now he was being interrupted. The irritation in his voice was noticed.

"Yes, Walt. I know and I apologize. I've been keeping a close eye on Margaret ever since she discovered the clue, but I don't think she's the one you want."

The schematic in Walt's hand lowered. That was news to him. "Oh? And why not? What do you mean?"

His visitor's throat was cleared. "As you know, the clue was pretty simple. Once she found the canister, I had the mermaids removed as you sug-

room for discussion or argument. The boss had spoken. "You know how to do that, right? To come back?"

"Yeah, Walt, I know how to do that."

Walt retook his chair and picked up the neglected blueprint. With that motion, his attention was back where it had been before the interruption and the interview was over. He failed to see the flash of anger as his entry door shut with a soft click.

Fullerton

Wolf stared at the photograph of the mermaids as they relaxed by the pool at the Disneyland Hotel after practice. Peter had unnecessarily pointed out which girl was his grandmother. Wolf remembered her from those days, but she wasn't the one who received his intense stare. He concentrated on the exotic-looking girl on the far right. Even though he had only seen her briefly at the darkened Park, he knew she was the same person he had chased. What confused him was that she appeared to be the same age now as when this photograph was taken. Could this be the daughter of the mermaid in the photo? Peter didn't seem to think so. He had seen her at least three times and was definite she was the same person.

As his mind whirled around the possible explanations—none of which seemed feasible—his attention was drawn to the noises Peter made as he worked on the mermaid from the Mansion. With Kimberly and Lance at work and the other two boys on a play date, Wolf had taken the opportunity to come to their house in Fullerton to see for himself what it was Peter had actually found. They had taken over the table in the dining room and pushed aside the elaborate flower arrangement.

Peter seemed determined to get that mermaid open—even if it meant taking a saw to it. Once Wolf heard that was one of Peter's options, he wisely vetoed that idea and told him to figure out another way.

"Gosh, this is like the Chinese water torture!" Without looking up, Peter continued to grumble in an undertone as he flipped the mermaid over yet again.

"You've never been in anything even close to a Chinese water torture. Do you even know what...."

Peter glanced up when Wolf suddenly went silent. "Do I know what what?" He protested when Wolf took the mermaid from his hands. "Hey, I was working on that."

The intense look that had been on Wolf's face slowly cleared as he stared at the girl. The confused thoughts and possibilities swirling through his mind seemed to come together as the girl was handed back to Peter. "It's just something you said. Something about the Chinese water torture."

"Should we put her under a dripping faucet until she opens?" Peter gave a laugh at his own joke without looking up to see his friend's reaction.

"No, not that." He paused again and looked at the little gold key on the table next to the clue. "Maybe we're thinking about this in the wrong way. The clue seems so simple that there must be something else to it. Possibly some kind of a puzzle."

"You mean like a word game?"

Wolf slowly shook his head back and forth.

"No, I don't think so. I was thinking more like a puzzle box. I saw a lot of them when I was in Chinatown."

"I don't understand. There's a puzzle hidden in a box somewhere? How do we find that without another clue?" Completely confused, Peter set the mermaid down and stared at Wolf.

"No. What I'm thinking is the box *is* the puzzle and the mermaid is the box. You have to move certain parts in a certain way to get it to open."

Peter looked at the redhead again. "But she's all smooth. Well, except for the pearls. And the scales on her tail. And, oh, her hair. You know what I mean."

"Did you check to see if any of those things actually moved?"

Peter began to get the sense of what Wolf was telling him and got a big grin on his face. "No. I was just trying to find a place to insert the key."

Wolf glanced at the grandfather clock in the corner. "I have to get back to the Park. Now that I have a new radio," he stopped to glare at the oblivious Peter, "I'd like you to call me if you find anything. Got it?"

"What? Call you? Sure."

When Peter happily got back to work and ignored him, Wolf gave a small smile. "I'll see myself out."

"**O**h, wow! The second pearl moved! Cool! Now what?"

Peter was elated when he was rewarded with the slight movement. He had pushed and prodded just about every square inch of the mermaid's body and had been ready to give up.

The pearl had only slid to one side a mere quarter of an inch. But that was all Peter needed to see a tiny button inside. The opening was so small that only the tip of the key would fit inside to push the nub. That slight depression of the button caused the index finger on her right hand to lift. Peter yelped in delight and eagerly reached for the key he had just set aside. But, looking closer, he didn't see the expected keyhole. Or another button to push.

"Now what? Did I break it?" He tried to move the finger up and down and it snapped shut again. "Uh oh. Better not do that again."

By repeating the first movements, the finger lifted again. As he tried to lift it back further and met resistance, he had to slow down and think about what he was doing. He didn't want to possibly break her hand. Moving the finger slowly side to side seemed to work as one of her eyes suddenly flipped up. "Eww. Catie wouldn't like that. Aww, no keyhole."

After gently trying to move the eye around with no results, Peter tried to push down on it. He heard a click and something nudged against his hand that held the green tail. One of the scales just below the waist had opened on a small hinge. "Bingo!" The keyhole was under that scale.

"I guess this is the key to the mermaid's tail. Hey, it was a word puzzle! The clue said it unlocked the mermaid's tale, not tail." Peter had the small key between his fingers, but he held back from inserting it and gave a sigh. "I'd better call Wolf first. He did make me promise."

Wolf held the radio away from his ear. "Peter. You're yelling. Say it again?"

Peter was in Lance's office. In perfect, unintended imitation of his dad, he had leaned back in the leather chair and had his feet up on the desk. "Wolf, it was so cool! I moved the pearl and it went to the side and I found a button but it was too small and I had to use the back of the key and it went 'ping!' and the finger lifted but it wasn't there so I tried to move it but it went back down but I got it to open again and then it was, like, 'squeak' and her eye popped out! It was so gross I was, like, eww! Then I moved the eye back and forth and I felt the scale open and it was in there!"

His enthused recital was met with silence. Wolf tried to sort out all the details he had just heard in one breathless rush. "Are you saying you got the mermaid to open?"

Peter made a sound that would have translated into 'duh.' "That's what I just told you! I found the place to turn the key!"

"What was inside?"

"Uh, I thought I had to call you first. I didn't open it."

Wolf gave a small smile. "Go ahead. Just let me know what you find. And, Peter? I want you to tell your parents about this before you do *anything*. Understand? I want you to promise me."

Peter knew better than to argue with him. He bit back a groan but knew Wolf couldn't see him roll his eyes. "Yes, sir."

"And, Peter?"

"What?"

"Don't roll your eyes at me."

Back in the dining room, key in hand, Peter again hesitated. "Wonder if I should wait for Catie and Alex to come home? They'd be disappointed it I opened it without them." Fairness warred against impatience over the discovery of the keyhole. Peter didn't know what he should do. The Michaels family wouldn't be home for at least four more days. That was, like, forever. A smile suddenly broke out on his face. "I could ask Catie if it was all right. She lets me do anything I want!"

Peter reluctantly set the key next to the mermaid and ran upstairs to his computer. He would send Catie a text and see what she said.

The answer came back almost immediately.

So excited!!!!!! Wait 4 me!!! No, wait, Alex says go ahead. :(Umm, Mom says hi. LOL

Peter stared at his computer screen. He didn't know which twin to go by. To play it safe, he texted Catie again. *Do I open it or not?*

Gosh, Peter, I said yes. LOL Wish I was there 2. Oh, Dad says get off phone. He is getting award now. Bye!!!!!!!!

"I guess that means yes." Peter clicked off the monitor and ran down the stairs to the first floor.

His heart beating in suspense, he found the little brass key fit perfectly into the lock. With a small twist, the locking mechanism that had kept its secret for fifty years popped open. The entire tail section proved to be hollow, but it wasn't empty. The item that had thudded inside the tail fell out onto the table and bounced off to the floor.

"Oh, gosh!" Peter hastily set the girl on the table and went to retrieve the fallen object. "Hope it's not broken. Hope it's not broken. Hope...."

with his latest find, it had taken an assurance from Wolf before Peter, Alex and Catie would be allowed to continue. Back from Missouri, Adam and Beth had been updated, as well. Once it was established that the entire security force would be alerted and available to keep an eye on their children—without their knowledge, of course—the go-ahead had been given. All three of the kids now were at Disneyland with the strict instruction to stay together at all times.

"What'd you say, Peter?" Alex turned back from the white spires of Space Mountain that were tempting him in the distance. He'd rather be on the roller coaster than at a standstill in the middle of To-morrowland.

Peter shook his head, frustrated. "Just thinking out loud, I guess. I can't figure out what the 268 means."

Catie had a suggestion. "We could ride the Monorail and see if there's any awning it goes under that we can't remember."

"Yeah, let's ride *something*. I mean, let's ride the Monorail."

"Gee, Alex, you could be a little more helpful."

"Hey, this clue-solving stuff is new to me." Good-natured like his dad, Alex just shrugged and didn't take offense. "I'm usually with Dad riding Screamin' while you guys do this clue stuff."

Screamin' sounded good to Peter, too, but he was on a mission. To make sure his crew didn't abandon him and force him to go back to his dad, he had to placate them. "Maybe later we can go over to California Adventure and ride the roller coaster. I'd really like to work on this a while longer." He looked over at his strongest ally and gave her a charming smile. "Is that all right, Catie?"

Alex gave a silent chuckle when he saw the admiration for Peter written all over her face. Restraining himself, he said nothing. He'd rather embarrass her in private.

"Sure, Peter! Whatever you say. Do you think it would be a good idea to ride the Monorail? We just missed that one, but I saw the orange one enter the Park."

"Hey, let's see if we can sit up front with the pilot!"

Glad to be doing something, the three friends raced up the ramp to the station and happily stood by the first entry gate to get their wish.

On the observation platform above the neighboring Autopia track, Wolf relaxed once they boarded the cockpit.

Seated at a corner table in the Tomorrowland Terrace restaurant, Omah knew she had about fifteen minutes to kill until they were back.

Alex longingly looked down from the curved front window of the Monorail into the California Adventure Park. He barely listened to the excited chatter of his two companions as they sped over the entrance to Soarin' Over California. That would have been fun, too.

"I think we need to concentrate just on Tomorrowland since the Monorail is based there. That's were most of the track is."

"But, Catie, we're on the track now and it's going over what used to be a parking lot and over to the Disneyland Hotel. Not to mention we just the way down the ramp. "So did you see anything that actually would help?"

Both twins just shook their heads no.

"Well, I have to go to the bathroom and I don't want to let Alex get too close to Space Mountain. So, let's head over to the one by Alice in Wonderland." Peter didn't wait for an answer and just started to walk in that direction. He heard a grumble from Alex something about a 'Fastpass and be done before Peter got out of the bathroom.' He had to stop, though, when Catie called him back and pointed at the Tomorrowland Terrace.

"Peter, while you're gone, we're going to get something to drink. We'll meet you by the White Rabbit."

Peter knew she referred to the large statue just beyond the restroom entrances. It used to stand by the exit of the Alice in Wonderland ride, but had been moved. It appeared to be permanently mounted on the wall of the ride's outer building. "We're supposed to stay together. Remember? That's the only way our parents let us come at all."

"So, you want Catie to go into the boy's room with you?"

At the girl's fierce blush, Peter waved his hand. "Hey, that's not what I meant and you know it! Fine. Get a drink. And get me a Coke while you're at it. I'll pay you back later."

As the twins headed back to the outdoor restaurant, Peter turned to walk past the Matterhorn Mountain. The next Monorail glided by on his right as it hugged the Mountain on its approach to the station. A hand waved out of one of the open windows.

Distracted by an incoming call, Wolf glanced

over as he came down the exit ramp of Autopia. When he spotted the twins' heads at the ordering counter, his attention returned to the radio.

With her hat pulled down to hide her red hair, Omah gave a smile when she saw the boy walk off by himself. "Gotcha now, Peter Brentwood."

"Hi, Uncle Wolf. You want some root beer?"

Wolf desperately tried to control the features on his face. He was about to start yelling when he realized Peter was not with the twins. "Where's Peter?" The words came out more forceful than he had intended.

Alex's eyes widened and the soda was lowered. "He...he went to the bathroom. Over by Alice. Is everything okay?"

I don't know if everything is okay. You're not together like you're supposed to be, are you? His mind shouted the words while his lips tried to give the kids a reassuring smile. "I'm sure everything's fine. Why don't we go find him, all right?"

Both heads nodded in unison as they followed the visibly-upset security guard.

"I told you you should've gone in with him, Catie."

"Eww. I'm not going in a boy's bathroom!"

"It was *your* idea to get a soda."

"What difference does that make?"

Wolf blocked out the mumbled argument as it continued behind him. Hand ready on the radio to call for back-up, he mentally chastised himself for letting the boy out of his sight. He had to hold himself from sprinting to the restrooms.

"See, Uncle Wolf? We made it here before

Forty years it took me. He laughed in my face when I asked him about it! Laughed at me!"

Peter knew she talked to herself right then. He desperately looked around for someone he could secretly signal that he was being taken against his will. He knew the dock ended but also remembered this woman had disappeared off of it somehow. He didn't want to end up in some long-forgotten tunnel—as cool as that might have been in other circumstances—with this obviously distraught woman. He thought he might be able to jerk his arm free, jump over the metal fence, swim to the bank and run through the nearby Autopia roadway to get away. As he went over his ambitious plan in his mind, his eyes shot upward when the Monorail quickly glided past. Maybe he could signal the pilot. No, the Monorail went by too fast. But, in that moment he saw something else and his mouth fell open.

"He finally told me I was crazy to still be looking for that stupid mermaid. Stupid, he called her! I was her model! Walt chose *me* for the mermaid's face." She turned unseeing, crazed eyes at the alarmed boy as they got to the end of the boat dock. "But I have to get her, you see. I promised Walt I would fix it. The captain told me if she was anywhere after all this time she would be in the Haunted Mansion. That was all he said and he threw me out of his house. As I left his porch he said the pearls go back to Constance. What pearls? The pearls on the mermaid were molded." She shook Peter again. "So, don't you see? I have to get the mermaid back to Walt. I have to show him I could do it. That I wasn't a failure."

Peter almost felt sorry for the woman. Since

her knife had not reappeared, he hoped he was past the danger mode and relaxed in her grip. "Uh, I don't know how to tell you this, but Walt's been gone for a long time."

Omah's eyes seemed to clear as she stared at him. She glanced down to where she tightly held his shirt and let go, yet still blocked the way out. "I know he's gone, Peter."

"You know my name!"

"Yes, I know your name and Catie's name. I've asked a lot of questions around here after you somehow got into the Mansion. You and your dad are pretty well known." She stopped and drew a deep, shuddering breath. All that emotion seemed to take everything out of her. "Listen, Peter, I just want the mermaid. And I'll do anything to get her. I...I have to get her back to Walt."

"That doesn't make any sense."

"Perhaps not to you, but it does to me. I don't care what you found inside her. I just want her back. Can we make a deal?"

Peter was wary, but pleased that she wanted to make a deal and not shove a knife into him. He was saved from any answer by the arrival of Wolf and the twins at the opening of the pier.

"Let the boy go, Omah."

At his sudden, deep voice, her eyes widened in surprise. "How do you know me?" She took a couple of steps back but ran up against the lean-to.

Peter tried to signal Wolf that he thought everything was all right. He didn't want to be caught in the middle of any cross-fire.

Wolf ignored the boy's not-too-subtle waving. "I know you were a mermaid in the Lagoon. I know some of your friends."

Anne pushed her white-rimmed sunglasses down her nose as she looked over at the blue-shuttered window of the ticket booth. "Ken, it's only twenty-five cents for another ticket. We don't get here very often. Let's just have fun. There's probably a lot to see as we go through the course."

As he got out his wallet, Ken looked over the dock and the three piers that jutted out into the green water. There were two boats docked for later use, one was blue and the other was red. "I'm sure it's just as good as that Mr. Toad ride. That was pretty fun!"

Ruth gave a little shiver. "I didn't like the train coming at us. That scared me!"

"Well, I can guarantee there won't be any trains coming at us on this ride!"

As they handed in their individual tickets, they wound through the near-empty line. A cast member dressed in a bold blue and white striped shirt and wide, white trousers had them wait at the opening as a green and white boat putted to a stop in front of them.

"I want a red one."

"Sorry, honey, this is ours. Careful. Hold onto Daddy's hand while I get in."

"Can I drive?"

Ruth scampered into the middle of the white seat and grabbed the steering wheel. Ken took the last space. Just as he sat, the small boat started moving past the remaining length of the dock and into the open channel. "Ruthie, honey, you could have waited until I was comfortable."

"Huh? Am I supposed to push on the pedal thingy down there?"

Anne looked down at her daughter's feet.

They were quite a ways away from the gas pedal. "Try it now, honey. Maybe once we get going you can drive it."

Ruth pushed hard on the metal pedal and could hear the engine *vroom*. Water churned out the back. "Here we go! Look! I'm steering!"

Anne looked over at Ken behind Ruth's back and shrugged. "I don't think we're moving any faster than we were. Do you?"

"Hey, Mom, there's those cars we drove. We're going under them! Why do they look like they're going faster than we are?"

"Because they probably are." Once they emerged from the bridge, Ken shaded his eyes against the glare of the bright sun sparkling off the water. Other than the overhead Autopia track and the Monorail track, there was no shade. "Try the gas pedal again, honey. It's kinda warm out here."

The engine sounded like it revved again and more water bubbled up behind them. "Here we go! Look! There's a lot of rocks up ahead. I'm going to steer really careful through there."

"You do that, honey. It is pretty back here, Ken. Lots of flowers and bushes."

Ken grunted as he fanned himself with the park guide they had gotten at the entry gate. "I didn't expect to pay another seventy-five cents for 'pretty.' I thought there'd at least be a waterfall or something to go over."

"What?" Ruth had been so concentrated on steering that she only half-heard what was said around her. "A waterfall? Like on the Jungle ride? Oh, you'd better steer, Daddy." Her hands flew off the wheel and she scooted the available inch closer to her mother. Her eyes immediately narrowed unheard. He felt he deserved to be in on the discussion since he was a Junior Guardian after all. Still, there was a hesitation to say anything just so he didn't inadvertently make it worse. When Lance and Wolf finally turned to him, he involuntarily took a step back. By the looks on their faces it could go either way.

"Okay, son, Wolf and I came to a decision." Lance paused, expecting Peter to jump in and defend himself before he heard what they had to say. When that didn't happen, he continued. "Okay, then. Alex, Catie, come on over here, please." He looked into each of the three eager, yet wary faces in front of him. "You all know we're worried about what keeps happening to Peter." They nodded, but remained silent, their eyes wide. "Well, we also know how important these treasure hunts are to you. They were important to me, too." He again stopped at the confused look that came over Alex's face. Apparently Peter hadn't told him about his dad's previous adventures. "Adam can fill you in later."

"Wait a minute. Dad was involved in something like this!? Is that what he was talking about in Missouri? When was that? What did he find?"

"Alex, we're getting off track here. What I was going to say is that you can finish what you started, but Wolf or I will be with you the whole time." Again the expected argument didn't come. Maybe the kids finally realized it isn't all fun and games. "Wolf will come with us right now because we think we need eyes and ears in more than just one place. Agreed?"

At the question the three kids quickly went into a huddle to discuss their options while the two adults watched, amused smiles on their faces. There seemed to be a lot of gestures and head-shakes with an occasional point at Wolf. When a mutual accord apparently had been reached, they broke apart. Peter, the elected spokesman, stood in front of his friends and announced that they were in agreement.

Lance bit back a smile at the stance Peter took. He was terribly proud of his son and couldn't wait to see how this would all work out—how Peter would continue to grow and develop. "Well, I'm glad to hear that. So, Peter, you said you figured out the clue. Where do we go?"

Glad they were being taken seriously, he pointed to the east. "Back to Fantasia Gardens, the old Motor Boat Dock."

Wolf bit back a groan. "I was afraid you were going to say that. Fine. Lance, you take the open-ing of the dock and I'll stand guard at the rear. She won't get past me again."

"**O**kay, this is what I found." Peter took the twins to the southern edge of the cement walkway. They could clearly hear the Autopia cars as they rumbled by on the other side of the thick, bushy bar-rier. Peter pointed up at the Monorail Track that curved away from them and followed the old Motor Boat channel below.

At least, the track was what the twins thought he meant. "What are we looking at, Peter? It's a cement beam like every other one in the Park."

"No, Alex, look under the beam, just at the top of the support thingy. See up there? What do you see?"

pull this bench over to the edge."

The scraping noise drew an inquisitive glance from Lance, but he remained where he was and let the kids figure it out. Wolf ignored them.

"Gosh, what do they make these benches out of? Cement? Is this far enough?"

"Yeah, set down your end, Alex." Peter hopped up on the wooden bench and touched the stiff fabric of the awning. It overlapped the roof and hung down a few inches past the corrugated metal of the cream-colored eaves. About every ten feet or so was a blue support beam that extended across the width of the roof and down the eaves. Peter ran his eyes across the ceiling, past the black light fixtures, to the other side. He could see no break in the metal that might be a hiding place. He did notice some old bird's nests that stuck out of the blue railing that extended the entire length of the roof.

"Hey, guys, look at that." He pointed at the various sticks and dried leaves moldering under the roof.

"Eww, that's gross. Don't touch it!"

"Catie, I wasn't going to touch it. I was just showing you there's room between that blue metal thing and the roof. Maybe what we are looking for is stuck in there."

"You want some gloves?"

"I'm not going to wear gloves! I'm just going to see if anything is crammed in up here."

"You think that might be it?"

"Maybe, Alex. I hope so." He gave a nervous glance toward the stroller parking area for Small World. "People are starting to stare again. We need to get done and get out of here. Catie, go tell my dad what I'm doing just so he doesn't have to come and look."

When the girl ran off, Peter cautiously stuck the tips of his fingers in the nook between the support rail and the overhang. He thought there might be some jagged edges on the metal and went slowly. With a check at the Monorail pillar in question, he tried to gauge how far he would need to explore before it encroached on the next pillar.

"Uh, Peter? You do know there's another rail just like it on the other side, too, right?"

"Oh, that's right. I forgot about that. Let me finish up here. I only found some dried sticks and dirt so far."

The kids drug the park bench over to the side of the dock closest to Its a Small World. The princess meet-and-greet in the pavilion closest to them was not in session, so the only guests were farther away in line for Small World. Peter repeated his first movements. Only this time his fingers came in contact with something harder than a stick.

"I think I found something!"

"What is it, Peter!?"

The answer came out in grunts. "It's really wedged in here. Pretty small." He rose on his tip-toes to try and peer into the track. "Whatever it is was painted over. It's all blue. Wait. I got a finger under the edge. Nope. Need a knife."

"I don't have a knife on me, Peter."

"I know that, Catie. Sheesh. Go ask my dad for something sharp or pointy."

A moment later Peter was handed a pen. "He said it was the best he could do."

"Hope he doesn't want it back in one piece." Peter went at the small stuck box like an explorer hacking his way through the jungle.

Alex and Catie stood back as blue paint chips and pieces of the pen rained down on them. "Gosh, Peter. Don't break it."

Peter was too intent on his mission to ask if Alex meant the pen or the canister. "Got it!" Peter jumped down from the bench and handed the remains of the pen to Catie. A small canister was held up in the air in triumph. It was blue on one side and gray on the other. "Woo hoo!" He danced around the Monorail pillar as the other two high-fived each other with big grins on their faces.

When it became obvious the search was over, Lance came to join them. He frowned at the shards of the pen Catie handed him. "Great. Thanks. Why don't you guys put the bench back in place and let's get out of here. We're getting way too much attention since Peter started yelling and jumping around. Wolf! Let's go."

With a shake to clear the water from his arm, Wolf stalked up to them. They knew not to ask if he found anything. It was clear the woman's escape route was still a secret. "You want to take them home now, Lance?"

A loud chorus of "Awwww" met his suggestion.

Lance raised an eyebrow at the kid's negative response. That was unexpected. "I thought you'd want to get home and open the canister."

"Umm, I kinda promised the twins we'd go over to California Adventure and ride Screamin'."

Alex eagerly nodded his agreement with Peter. Ready to have some fun now that he felt the search was over, he wasn't too interested in the contents of the small box.

"I'd rather go on Ariel." Not overly fond of the fast, twisting roller coaster, Catie's face had fallen.

Wolf heard her low mumble that had been ignored by everyone else. "I'll go on Little Mermaid with you, Catie."

She looked up at him in surprise. "You will? I didn't think you'd like rides like that."

He put an arm around her shoulder as they headed for Main Street and the main gate. He didn't care about riding anything right then, but had seen the stricken look on her face. She shouldn't be forced to ride something she wasn't ready for yet. "I *love* the Little Mermaid. Plus, it fits your treasure hunt."

"Yeah, you're right. We have a redhead mermaid and Ariel is redhead, too." She warmed up to Wolf now that she felt he understood her fears and became chatty. "Peter and I talked about that in the Mansion when we found her. He thought the mermaid might be Ariel, but I didn't think so. Her face was all different."

Wolf looked down when she stopped walking and saw the frown on her face. "What's wrong?"

"Hmm?" She looked up him, obviously trying to figure something out. "Oh, I was just thinking about the mermaid we found. She...she kinda looks like that woman chasing us. Do you think what she told Peter was true? That she was the model? Shouldn't she be old like you or something?"

Wolf thought back to what Peter had said about the woman's ranting. "Yeah, or something. I don't know, Catie. I need to talk to her myself." *And I plan on doing just that.*

Catie gave a little shudder. She didn't want to be there when that interview took place.

CHAPTER 8

Omah paced her den. The more she paced, the angrier she became. Yellowed, water-stained newspapers were crushed underfoot as she strode back and forth, back and forth across the small, dimly lit room.

"That meddling boy! Why did he have to be so…so stubborn! I poured my heart out and he didn't believe me. Was I being unreasonable? Was I being demanding? No! Stupid, stupid boy. I just want the mermaid back."

A colorful brochure mixed in with the ragged papers caught her eye and she moved the sodden heap aside with her foot. It was a Disneyland guide map given to all the guests as they entered the main gate. This one announced the Park's Tencennial Celebration in 1965, Disneyland's ten year anniversary—and the year the mermaids came back to the Submarine Lagoon.

Omah abruptly sat next to the brochure and stared at it. 1965. It had been such a good year, such a promising one. Her position with Walt was secure. Her decision to join the mermaids to fulfill

Kimberly took advantage of the diversion to brush the rest of the soil on her fingers onto the back of her pants. She flashed Lance a wide, innocent smile when he saw her movement. "So, tell me, what did you find? Did you solve the clue? You guys hungry?"

Lance gave a wry smile at her subterfuge and joined the chorus of, "We're starved!"

"You're always hungry." Kimberly slipped her arm around Lance's waist as they all trooped into the house.

Lance let her have her diversion. He already knew about the holes out back. It didn't take a genius to figure out they really didn't have so much of a gopher problem as a Dug problem. "Say, Pete, show your mom the canister you found."

"Oh, you did find one! It's so odd that this clue wasn't on the...." She abruptly broke off when Alex and Catie turned to stare at her, curiosity written all over their faces. They didn't know about the War Room on the third floor of the Brentwood's house or their roles as Guardians of Walt Disney. She and Lance had discussed the possible reasons this Hidden Mickey quest hadn't been on the large holographic map of the Disney world. Whenever a clue was found, a green blinking light turned red to alert the Guardians on watch. They would then make sure everything was followed as it should be and that no harm came to Walt's carefully-laid plans. Her father had been one of Walt's right-hand men and was, with Wolf, the first of the Guardians to see that Walt's legacy continued as Walt had wanted. Kimberly shot a pleading look at Lance to come to her assistance. It wasn't up to them to tell Catie and Alex. The twin's parents didn't even know the whole story—and they had been in on the initial find that had started it all. She started to flounder. "Umm, the clue wasn't on the…."

"Wasn't on the Mark Twain dock like I thought." Lance winked at her as he took a bite of meat and cheese she had prepared for them.

She gave him a grateful look and took his lead. "Oh? Not on the Mark Twain dock? Then where was it?"

Confused, Peter looked back and forth at his parents during this strange exchange. The possibility of the Mark Twain dock being the right answer had never even come up in discussion. That location wouldn't even have been *close* to being right. He opened his mouth to correct them but caught Lance's subtle shake of his head and his nod indicating Catie and Alex. "Oh, right. Yeah, NOT the Mark Twain. Yeah, wow, you were WAY off on that one, Dad!" Lance raised an eyebrow and Peter knew he'd better get off that track. "Mom, it was so cool! We found it at Fantasia Gardens. You know, the old Motor Boat Dock. It was wedged up under the awning where all the birds build their nests. Here, look at this!" He dug the small canister out of his backpack and handed it to his mom. "They actually painted over it! Nobody even knew it was there!"

Kimberly eagerly examined the thick plastic container. It still thrilled her every time a new one was discovered. Walt Disney actually touched this and put it into place! How she wished she could have met the man. Her father had told her so many stories of the decades they had worked together, but it wasn't the same. It wasn't the same as meeting him for yourself.

"You guys ready to open it?"

The rousing cheers were somewhat muffled by cheese and crackers but still enthusiastic.

With a strong desire to tear it open herself—with her teeth, if necessary—she quickly handed the case back to Peter. "Well, let's get it open."

Peter experienced the same thrill as his mom. Hand on the end cap of the small, round canister, about ready to twist, he remembered he wasn't alone on this search. Again his eagerness warred with fairness as he looked up at the eager faces around him. "Catie, I think it's your turn to open one. Alex got the last one." He even gave a small smile as he handed the treasure over to his friend.

The quiet anticipation was broken when Kimberly slapped her forehead. "Gosh, I was so excited about all of this I forgot. We need to tell your parents you're back from the Park."

"I'll go do it, Aunt Kimberly." All eyes turned to Alex at his volunteer. The unexpected attention caused him to take a step back. "What!?"

"We just thought you'd like to see what's inside, that's all."

He could tell by the looks on everyone's faces that they expected him to be as eager as they were over this treasure thing. "Oh, yeah. I do, but, uh, Michael said he was going to show me his new game console. I can call Dad from upstairs. Is that okay?"

Surprised that Alex wasn't interested in what might be another clue, Lance let the two boys go. He already knew Michael had no desire to be part of this quest just like he had opted out of the first one with Peter. Young Andrew, as expected, took off with the older boys and Dug bounded up the stairs behind the trio. "Well, *I* want to see what's inside. Go ahead, Catie."

Catie slowly turned back from watching Alex leave the room. She had always known he wasn't as keen on Disneyland as she was, but this...this was exciting! *How could he not want to see what was inside?* With a small, disappointed shrug, she got to work to open the half blue, half gray canister.

"Mermaids seem to come in threes.
Is yours a sister to one of these?
With plenty of sparkles and hair of gold,
There's more of this Tale yet to be told."

"Small canister, small clue. What?" Lance handed the yellowed paper back to Peter's eager hands as he questioned the unsure look that slowly spread over Kimberly's face.

So they couldn't hear her, she turned away from the two kids who were busy examining the small golden screwdriver that had fallen out with the clue. With a lowered voice, she leaned closer to Lance. "I just don't remember Walt being so...so poetic in any of the previous quests. It wasn't like him. Do you really think he's the one who set this up? Could that be why none of these locations showed up on the map in the War Room?"

Lance gave a slow shake of his head while he thought about what her words implied. He hadn't considered the possibility it might not be from Walt. "The handwriting looks right. We'd have to compare it with the clues we saved upstairs." He stopped talking and turned to look out the kitchen window.

"What?"

Now his face mirrored her uncertainty. "Wolf didn't know anything about this quest. He and your father had worked with Walt to set all the others in place. But this one is as much a puzzle to Wolf as it is to Peter and the twins." Before Kimberly could comment, his face suddenly broke out in a wide smile. "Maybe Wolf isn't as all-seeing, all knowing as we thought!"

His smile broke the tension and she visibly relaxed. "And maybe Walt had a few secrets up his sleeve."

Lance pulled his wife in for an impromptu hug. "There's that possibility, too. It does add an aura of mystery to this quest."

"Dad! Eww. We have company."

"Lance, did you just use the word aura?"

Lance gave Kimberly a quick kiss before she could pull loose. "Never you mind, son. So, what do you think the clue means? Where do you go next?"

Peter's answer was interrupted when Alex bounded down the stairs, Dug barking at his feet. "Catie, Mom says we need to come home! You forgot to do your homework."

"Aww, I was going to do it tomorrow! We have all day Sunday. Hey, we got the box thing open, Alex! Do you want to see the clue?"

"Oh. More mermaids. Great." Alex abruptly handed the paper back to his sister. "Yeah, that's…uh…cute. Uncle Lance, do you want Dad to come get us? I'm supposed to call him right back."

If they hadn't known for sure by his actions before, it was now completely obvious that Alex wasn't into this whole quest thing. Lance recalled how excited Adam had gotten with each new discovery during their search. *Well, to each his own*, he thought. *People have to follow their own path.* "Why don't we all drive you home? We need to let your mom and dad know the latest, anyway. It'll be a good chance to catch up."

Kimberly looked at him with narrowed eyes. "Catch up, huh? You just talked to Adam this morning."

Lance chose to ignore her reminder. "Michael, go get your little brother. Peter, put a leash on that mongrel and get her in the van. I'll put the Jag in the garage and we'll be all set."

"What are you up to?"

Lance gave his wife the charming smile that had gotten him out of scrapes for decades. It didn't work. "Nothing, sweetheart. Just paying a friendly visit to old friends."

"Lance, its dinnertime. It isn't right for the whole family to just show up like that."

His face was all innocence. "It is? Hadn't noticed. Besides, Adam owes me a meal. He missed the last putt on the eighteenth hole."

"Owes *you* a meal. We are five, in case you forgot how to count."

With a regal wave of his hand, Lance dismissed her objections. "Five. One. It's all the same. You guys ready? Let's get going! I hear a steak calling me!"

Adam had to stand back from his doorway as more people than he expected trooped into his house. Typically unfazed by most events, he did raise an eyebrow when Dug gave an excited, high-

"Well, it is serrated on the sides, but it does feel a bit thinner to me."

"Yeah, that's what I thought, too."   Adam's voice began to get more excited and enthused. "You know, we could pull out those old Disneyland books of yours and start researching mermaids at the Park. Are they in the library or the extra room upstairs?"

"Mom! Dad!"

Adam and Beth looked up from the clue at the shrill voice. Catie stood staring at them, hands on her hips, Peter right beside her. "What?" They looked back and forth at the disapproving looks obvious on the kids' faces. "What's wrong? What's with the attitude?"

Eyes wide, Catie hadn't expected that response and looked to Peter for support. At his slight nod, she cleared her throat. "We…we would rather do this by ourselves."

Adam glanced over at Lance and Kimberly and got a 'that's what we got, too' look. "Oh, I see. I thought that's why you brought it all over. That mermaid is pretty cool."

"We just wanted to show you, not have you solve it, Dad."

"Okay. I understand. Just like that time, I guess." He could see the two kids visibly relax when he handed the clue back to Catie. "But, if you need any help or want to use any of Mom's books, go ahead."

Glad to see her dad understood, Catie gave him a wide smile. "Thanks, Dad. Come on, Peter. Let's go to my room and see what we can find on the computer."

"They're getting so big." Beth gave a wistful

sigh as they ran off. "Can't believe the twins are eleven already."

Adam gave his wife a hug. "So, Lance, I take it their search was uneventful this time." He felt Beth shudder slightly in his arms. They both still worried about the possible threat of that woman Omah and wondered if they did the right thing in letting it continue.

The smiles and friendly feelings vanished like morning dew in the hot sun. Lance nodded, serious again. "Even though the entire security force is on alert, Wolf and I both went with them to the old boat dock. We won't take any chances. Peter, for some reason, thinks she really doesn't want to hurt him. But, like I said, we aren't taking any chances."

"We sure didn't have this problem when we were doing our Hidden Mickey quests. It's odd it's happening to Peter and Catie."

Lance gave a laugh. "No problems? Adam, you jumped off the steam train in the big tunnel and rappelled into the little caverns. And the three of us jumped out of the boat in Pirates of the Caribbean and hid behind the bed in the Captain's Quarters!"

"Well, *we* didn't have anyone chasing us." Beth glanced over at Kimberly. "But you had your uncle after you, and what about Nimue?" She then looked Lance straight in the eye. "Are you sure you and Wolf have this handled? Will the twins and Peter be safe?"

With the understanding of a parent, Lance repeated his earlier assurance to the worried Adam and Beth. "Wolf and I will do everything we can to keep them safe. You know that, Beth." He felt Kimberly slip her hand into his for a quick, reassuring squeeze. "We don't want anything to happen to at the large moose but could see nothing out of the ordinary. "Gosh, might as well be in the Haunted Mansion."

The steady water current pushed her into the entrance of the large gold and white, sparkling façade of Its a Small World. A cold blast of air hit her in the face as the brilliant sunlight began to fade. On a hot summer day the refreshing air would be a welcome relief from the Southern California heat. This air, however, wasn't so inviting. It felt….a little more menacing to the girl who hugged her arms as goose-bumps broke out. The familiar welcome signs lining the banks were dull and dark. The glitter and sequins that covered them caught an occasional glint of light and gave off a feeble wink of color in the darkness. The familiar Small World song she wanted to sing along with could not yet be heard.

A trickle of fear started to send shivers down Catie's spine when the little boat rounded the next corner. The warm, colorful lighting for each display was turned off and, instead, the stark industrial overhead lighting made everything look dull and flat. The beautiful costumed dolls were in different clusters than their usual arrangements. It was as if they were in the middle of a deep discussion when she intruded. Dressed in white costumes of Iceland and Denmark, one group had their arms crossed as they surrounded the figures from Spain and England. The can-can dancers had tight hold on ropes that held the soaring kites straining overhead—and they didn't look too happy about it. One of the girl's pink-feathered headdress was broken and hung off to the side. Next to them, the sparkling tiger from Siam was crouched low to the ground as it watched the Antarctica penguins. Circled around the out-of-place penguins, yellow hyenas from the Africa scene rocked back and forth and appeared to be silently laughing at the little birds' dilemma.

Worried, Catie turned in her seat to look for the next boat behind her. She needed the reassurance that somebody, anybody else was there and everything was all right. Only, there was no other boat behind her. The channel was empty.

"I'm safe at Disneyland. I'm safe at Disneyland. Nothing will hurt me. They're only dolls." She made the words play over and over in her mind as her strange voyage continued. Instead of going in their usual circles, some of the figures danced in a straight line as if they were on their way to the next room. A few were perched on the edge of the channel like they were attempting to get in the boat with her. "I'm safe. They're only rearranging the displays. I got in here by mistake. That's why the music is off."

Crouched down on the floor of the boat now, Catie anxiously peered from below the silver hand rail. As the boat traveled forward, the overhead lights began to flicker on and off. "Please don't go out," she whispered, her voice pleading. "Please don't go out. This is the happiest crew that ever sailed the seas. This is a happy crew. Please...."

As the small boat bumped around the next corner, the large pink hippo turned its head to look at Catie as it entered the room. The rhinoceros beating on the blue and pink drum stopped to look at the fuzzy monkey high above its head. Before the monkey could respond, the elephant lifted its trunk and let out a loud trumpet. It was the first noise she had heard above the mechanical clicking and

whirring of the dolls' movements—and it was terrifying. Were they alerting the others that she was
coming?

Heart pounding, Catie ducked her head down
as the treacherous lights flickered one more time
and finally went out. But it wasn't completely dark.
There were odd glowing lights from different flowers
on display and even the eyes of some of the ani-
mals were lit from within.

"Please come back on! Come on, lights. I
need you."

Catie's favorite scene was next but she was
too afraid to enjoy it. One of the koala bears had
gotten into the kangaroo's pouch and the bright blue
platypus was hanging onto the sequined sun. The
green and yellow sea turtles had come down from
their wires to protectively surround the three mermaids who huddled in a group behind the seaweed
backdrop. The beaks of the turtles snapped at the
girl when she dared to peek out to see where she
was.

Just before she could duck back down again,
Catie saw the heads of all the dolls and all the ani-
mals suddenly turn to the right. All their sporadic
movements stopped. Those who had been on the
march immediately froze in place and the turtles
moved closer to the frowning mermaids.

Scared as she was, Catie was also so mes-
merized that she had to see what they saw. Her
head turned of its own accord to follow their gazes.
Her breath caught in her throat as a pair of sharp
blue eyes peered around the edge of the South
Seas entry. These eyes weren't like the round, life-
less eyes on the figures. These were living eyes,
blinking, staring, real eyes…and they were now fol-

lowing the movement of Catie's boat.

Only then did she realize her boat wasn't moving forward any longer. The flowing water had stopped and her boat wasn't inching any closer to the grand finale room. After that room was the longed-for exit where she knew she could get out into the welcome sunlight and safety. She scooted over to the edge of the boat as far away as possible from those evil blue eyes and made a frantic, feeble attempt to paddle the water with her hands. Anything to get the boat moving again.

It didn't work. The boat stayed where it was as if it was anchored to the bottom of the bright blue flume.

"I know you, girl."

She heard the voice that came from the direction of those piercing eyes. Reluctantly she looked back. She had no choice. Her head turned back toward the sound.

"I know you. I know what you want. Do you hear me, girl?"

As Catie's hand came up to her throat, the blue eyes blinked and could not be seen any longer. A moment of relief washed over her. Maybe it was gone. Whatever *it* was.

Maybe…. No, there the eyes were again, only closer to the circle of turtles which hissed. The lights flickered on for a brief moment and Catie immediately wished they hadn't.

On the bank she saw a wolf. Not the warm, fuzzy, feather-covered kind that she expected to see on this ride. This wolf wasn't blue or pink or yellow. It didn't have pastel flowers covering its hide. This wolf was real. Its coat was a deep red with a thick undercoat of black hairs. The black out-

the kind, brown eyes of her mother. "Wolf."

"You were dreaming about Uncle Wolf?" Beth sat on the edge of Catie's rumpled bed and ran a soothing hand over the girl's hair. She had never before seen her daughter so distraught. "You're okay, honey. Everything's okay now."

Hearing her mother's calming voice, Catie gave a little whimper and scooted closer. "It was a bad dream."

"Yeah, I kinda figured that. You want to tell me about it?" Her hand kept up its soothing motion and moved to the girl's back.

"I was on It's a Small World at Disneyland."

Beth gave a small giggle. "I think your brother would agree that would be terrifying."

The unexpected humor seeped into Catie's consciousness and helped her to relax. She gave a half-hearted laugh that came out as a snort. "It was, like, so silly, Mom. I was on a boat all by my-self and all the dolls were, well, weird. And then a wolf came out of the background and talked to me."

"A talking wolf? Now that's weird. I don't re-member any wolf in Small World."

"It was a real wolf, not a doll." She shook her head as if to clear the images out of her mind. She lifted her strained face to her mother. "Can I sleep with you and Daddy tonight?"

Beth gave her a tight hug. "Sure you can, honey, until you have to get up for school. Just tell yourself it was only a dream, okay?"

As Catie followed her mother to the master bedroom, she tried to do just that.

But the images wouldn't leave her mind.

Later that afternoon, while Catie and Alex finished up some homework, their parents had a serious, private discussion.

"Do you think the kids have had too much trauma? Could this be why Catie had that nightmare? It's not like her to have bad dreams like that."

"I don't know, Beth. I know she's been worried about that woman following Peter, but I thought she was more excited than scared. Wouldn't she have come to us if it was too much for her?" Adam ran a hand through his wavy hair. He wasn't sure what to do. "We both know these treasure hunts Walt left in place are exciting, but they aren't supposed to be dangerous." He paused and looked back at his wife. One possible decision that ran through his mind probably wouldn't go over very well with either Catie or Peter. He gave a sigh before he voiced his thought. "Maybe we should pull the plug on this Hidden Mickey search. Or finish it ourselves for them."

Beth took a deep, calming breath. Their dog Sunnee wandered over and pushed Beth's hand up so she would scratch her golden head. Beth automatically patted the dog without realizing it. "That would probably break their hearts. Would *you* have wanted someone to step in and pull the plug?"

Adam lowered his voice and looked around even though he knew the kids weren't close enough to hear. "Well, we did have a gun pointed at us toward the end. But, we were adults, not eleven and thirteen."

"You know Lance would never have shot us." Beth gave a sigh. A treasure hunt—even when the end result isn't definite—can do odd things to people. "But, I understand your point. Kimberly still has scars on her arm from when her uncle attacked her trying to take her treasure away from her." She bent down to give the dog a hug and was rewarded with a sloppy kiss on the cheek. "I just don't want our kids scarred—physically or emotionally."

"None of us do, honey. I'm sure Lance and Kimberly would agree with us on that. But, how would Peter and Catie feel if we made them stop?" Adam left out a frustrated breath of air. "I don't know. Think we should talk it over with the Brentwoods before we make a final decision?"

"Tomorrow is Saturday. The kids will probably want to go back to the Park to follow up on that next clue." She stopped for a moment and frowned. "They did figure out the next step, didn't they?"

Adam shrugged and gave a small smile. "I'm not in that loop. Why don't we head over to the Brentwood's house so we can talk to them in person?"

Beth glanced up at the clock. "Now? It's dinnertime."

Adam gave a wicked grin. "Yeah, I know. Just like Brentwood did to us last week.

Peter was fascinated as Catie described her dream to him with much hand waving and gestures. When she got to the part about the wolf, he had to interrupt. "Was it a huge black wolf with silver tips on his hair? And blue eyes and a white spot in the middle of his chest?"

Catie was a little taken aback. The nightmare had really scared her and Peter sounded all eager about the wolf. "It wasn't black, Peter! Gosh, you sound like you're describing Uncle Wolf if he actually turned into an animal. Sheesh! It was a red wolf—and really scary!"

"Uhm, a red wolf. Oh. Okay." Peter planted a wide, guilty smile on his face. *How could I be so stupid? She doesn't know about Uncle Wolf.* "Sorry. Go ahead."

"I...I told you most of it. It was just so weird. There were some explosions and I escaped." She frowned at the stupid look on Peter's face, but figured he wouldn't tell her where he got his idea of a black wolf. She let the dream drop and turned to something that they both equally worried about. "Do you think our parents will let us continue with this treasure hunt?"

The odd smile on his face faded. Peter nervously fiddled with a pen as he sat at his desk. "I think so. Don't know why a silly dream would make them tell us to stop." He could see a hurt expression flicker over Catie's face as she sat on the floor across from him. "I mean, it was scary, but why would we have to quit?"

She gave a helpless shrug. "Maybe I shouldn't have told them. Mom heard me yell out or something and came in my room."

Peter picked up the yellowed riddle from the pile on his desk. He gave her a wide grin as he held the paper out in front of him. "It might have been a little scary, but you did figure out the next location."

Catie brushed the paper from in front of her face. "I know what the clue says." She sounded irritated. "You don't have to wave it in my face. What did I figure out?"

The clue was dropped back on the desk. He

asked another question rather than answer her. "How many mermaids did you see in your dream?"

"Everyone knows there are three in that scene. Ariel is now in the middle on top and two more are down below. But, there're also three mermaids in the Peter Pan ride."

"But the mermaids in Peter Pan weren't there in Walt's time. I found out in my research that they were added a lot later. The three mermaids in Small World have been there a long, long time." He purposely quit talking to let it sink in and leaned back in his chair to watch the expression on her face.

The pique on her face slowly was replaced by the dawning of understanding. Her mouth formed a small O as she thought about it. "And the whole ride is covered with sparkles and glitter! Which one has golden hair?"

Glad to see she didn't stay mad at him, Peter eagerly leaned forward. "I saw some pictures and the one on the bottom right has yellow hair. That has to be the golden hair. Ariel's is red and the other one has either brown or black hair. They aren't sparkly, but the seaweed behind them is. Maybe we have to search the seaweed."

Catie's enthused expression dulled. "But how do we get to the seaweed? Unless we find the ride shut down like Mansion was, the boats go by in a steady stream."

"Yeah, there is that." Peter hadn't yet figured out that part. During their first treasure hunt, he had had to jump out of the Pirates of the Caribbean boat to get away from the thief. But, those boats were spaced a ways apart. Catie was correct. The boats in Small World usually caught up to each other and were a tight line. How could they manage to get off the boat unseen? And then there was the problem of the hidden cameras. "I could try and find where Mom hid the Key to Disneyland. Wolf told her to put it in a safer place." *Traitor*, his mind added.

"What if there was some kind of diversion in the next boat behind us and it didn't take off from the loading dock when it should? Would that give us enough time?"

"Depends on the diversion." Peter tapped the pen on his school binder as he thought. "We'd have to get someone else to help us. Unless one of us went alone to find the next clue and the other one caused the diversion." Seeing her eyes go wide, Peter knew he would have to go with his first suggestion. Catie wouldn't be comfortable with either role of causing the diversion or going by herself. "Do you think Alex would be willing to help us?"

Catie just remembered something and groaned. "That sounds good, but our parents said we can't go alone any more. At all. How would we pull this off with Uncle Wolf or Mom or Dad with us?"

Peter's shoulders slumped. "Oh, yeah. I forgot. If we get to go at all." He looked toward the door to his bedroom. "You think they're done talking about us yet? Should we go find out?"

Reluctance was obvious on her face. "I don't know what I'll do if they say no."

"Yeah. Me, either." He stood from his chair and took a deep breath. "Well, we might as well go find out. You ready, Partner?"

Hearing him call her that, Catie perked up and gave him a beaming smile. Whatever happened, she still had that. "Partner."

CHAPTER 10

"**P**eter, will you *please* quit pouting?"

The close-knit group of six slowly wound their way through the busy queue of It's a Small World. Arms tightly folded across his chest, Peter hung back from the two sets of parents, ever-loyal Catie by his side. "Don't see why all of us have to go."

"I expected that attitude from Catie, not Peter." Adam had to hide a grin behind his hand as he mumbled to his wife. Before he turned to the sullen boy he managed to straighten out his face. "Hey, I'm not thrilled to have to ride this either, but it's what we discussed last night."

"After Catie's bad dream, you went along with the decision that we would all ride with her the first time." Personally, Lance agreed with the reason behind Adam's lack of enthusiasm, but he also knew the adults had to present a united front. If the kids sensed any sign of weakness, they would pounce. Once Peter and Catie figured out how to find the next clue, the group would break up and help them accomplish whatever they needed to do. He also knew Wolf was stationed at the back of

Small World's show building, watching the exits and keeping an eye out for Omah.

Peter let out an unconvinced huff of air and glanced sideways at Catie to see what she thought about all of this. He discovered that her eyes were wide and her face betrayed an air of anxiousness as she stood closer to him than she usually did. "It'll be okay, Catie." Realizing how hard she was trying to hide her distress, he finally relaxed his obstinate stance to help with her needs. A dream's only a dream but she obviously took this one seriously. "We'll make sure nothing bad happens."

At the sound of his voice next to her ear, Catie broke out of her trancelike stare. She had fixated on the boatloads of guests who bumped around the narrow channel on their way into the attraction. After a tiny shiver, she gave a small nod and tried to smile. "I know. I'm just being stupid."

Peter put an arm up to give her a hug, but let it drop back to his side instead. *No need to get mushy.* "You're not stupid. You're just a girl!"

The jibe worked as she gave his arm a punch. Seeing his grin, she knew he was just teasing her. The anxious lines on her face disappeared when she gave him a smile that was tinged with a little competitive spirit. "Just a girl, huh? Well, we'll just see who finds the next clue first, won't we?"

Listening in without appearing to be listening, the parents gave a silent, united sigh of relief. Worried about Catie, they all were glad to see her return to her usual cheerful self. Plus, they were tired of Peter's cranky attitude.

"Can Catie and I at least have the front row of the boat to ourselves?"

"You want us all to huddle in the fifth row,

buddy? I know! We can pretend we don't know you."

Peter looked as if he was seriously considering his dad's option. Then he noticed the looks on the faces of the other adults and rolled his eyes. "Fine. Just don't…suffocate us."

"Okay. Adam, put away the leashes and collars. Beth, quit hovering. Kimberly, put the pepper spray back in your purse. They want to do this themselves. Kids. Sheesh."

The parents chuckled amongst themselves while Lance continued to hand out his instructions. Peter gave a snort and shook his head at Catie. *Adults. Sheesh.* When they boarded their flat-bottom boat, he glanced back and realized they had two rows of strangers behind them. Scooted companionably close, Lance had his arm around Kimberly's shoulder in row four. Back in row five, Adam and Beth had their heads together and were whispering into each other's ears.

"**M**an, how long is this ride? Aren't we there yet?"

"Gosh, Peter, quit complaining! I could have brought Alex if I wanted to hear that." Catie considered hitting him in the arm again as she resumed humming the recurring theme song. "Why do you think Alex and your brothers chose to go swimming at Grandma Margaret's instead of coming with us?"

"We need the clue. We need the clue. We need the clue." Peter kept up his mantra as the song continued—both around him and next to him, thanks to Catie. "Why couldn't Walt have hid it inside Space Mountain?"

Catie turned back to him and couldn't help but grin. She had heard every mumbled word. "There wasn't any Space Mountain way back then and you know it! The South Seas section is just after this one."

"Finally."

"No, the finale is in the room after that one!"

"I said finally, not finale."

"I know. Just quit mumbling!" She gave a light giggle and turned back to the bright piñatas of Mexico. A group of ruffled dancers were circling under a huge sombrero. There was a low growl that came from Peter but he otherwise remained silent.

"Finale," he smiled as the shimmering blue lights that gave the impression of being underwater came into view. Ariel had the top center position of the three mermaids and sea turtles bobbed on their lines on either side of her. "There's our golden-haired mermaid, Catie." His voice betrayed his excitement as he unnecessarily pointed out the doll on the left of the bottom row. "There's a lot of seaweed behind them. Looks like some good walls to hide behind, too. We need to get back there."

"You think there's an exit out the back somewhere close? Gosh, we passed it already! Do we need to ride again?"

The two kids turned in their seats to look back as the boat continued its voyage into Australia. When the mermaids could no longer be seen, they turned forward again, oblivious to the rest of the ride. Heads together, voices low, they discussed possible ways to get behind the seaweed.

"Did you see how close the next boat was, Peter?"

"Yeah, we'd never be able to jump without

being seen."

"What other way do we have? How do we make sure there's no boat behind us?"

Peter's thumb jerked back over his shoulder. "Maybe our parents can finally help. What if your mom and dad caused some kind of delay at the dock so the next boat didn't take off right away? And then my mom and dad could do something loud and obnoxious in the front of our boat so we could jump out of the last row. Do you think that would work?"

"What in the world would your mom do that was obnoxious?"

Peter gave a wide smile. "That would be left up to my dad."

"Oh, we're outside already. I always loved that lion."

"What lion? What are you talking about?"

Catie pointed up on the bank above them on their right. A topiary lion proudly sat on the grassy lawn, his body a tight-cropped green and his mane a wild profusion of a brown bush.

They were silent with their thoughts as the train blew its whistle twice and pulled out of the nearby Toontown Station. Steam coming out of its black smokestack, the bright red *Ernest S. Marsh* chugged through the façade of Small World as it headed for Tomorrowland. Some of the guests seated in the green and white canopied cars waved at the people down below.

Once the group was gathered in the shade of the nearby Small World Toy Shop, Lance radioed for Wolf to join them.

"I think we need to ride it one more time."

Catie's suggestion was instantly met with a loud chorus of four male voices. "No!"

"But...."

"No!"

"We'll figure it out, honey." After Adam gave her a reassuring pat on the shoulder, he turned to Kimberly. "Do you need to check in with my mom to see how the kids are doing? You said Andrew wasn't feeling well. I don't know how long we'll have to be here today."

Beth gave a knowing smile. "I think Margaret is happy playing Grandma Michaels to all the kids."

"Well, if you want me to drive you all the way to Yorba Linda to check on Andrew, let me know."

"Gee, that was heart-felt, Lance. Thanks."

Lance waved Adam off. "You know what I mean. I personally think the boys just didn't want to have to ride Small World over and over."

Kimberly knew Lance's assessment of Andrew's health was pretty accurate but still took her phone out of her purse as the discussion continued around her. They were all so intent on what they were doing that they failed to hear a startled gasp come from around the curve of the toy shop.

Dressed in a blonde wig, light-toned makeup, and huge sunglasses, Omah pressed herself flat against the side of the building. Pieces to her on-going puzzle had just fallen into place and she had to place a hand over her mouth to keep any other exclamations from accidentally escaping.

"Margaret is Margaret Michaels. I knew that. So, she is grandmother to the girl Catie. Then, that

must be Margaret's son and daughter-in-law. That's what I couldn't figure out. How Catie figured into all this. Margaret must have given them the clue she found back in 1965." Omah had to force herself not to pace as she continued to whisper. She didn't want to catch the attention of that sharp-eyed security guard. "*Wolf!*" she snorted. "*If he only knew!*" Her hand clamped tighter on her mouth as her shoulders shook with sudden uncontrolled laughter. When other guests passing by began to stare at her odd movements and whisperings, she made an effort to control herself. Her piercing, challenging stare back at them caused the guests immediately to move on.

"*Maybe Margaret knows where my mermaid is.*" Omah looked at the nearby gold and white pillar at the corner of the building. From what she could hear, the discussion was winding down and she needed to move away from the group. Even though she had managed to outwit Wolf so far, she didn't want to press her luck. "*Yorba Linda, huh? Maybe I need to pay a long-overdue visit to my dear friend Margaret.*"

Careful to move casually like the rest of the guests around her, Omah walked away and blended in with a tour group who had just gotten off the ride.

As she strode off with a park map held up to conceal her face, Wolf's head jerked in that direction. He had caught a whiff of scent on the light breeze but couldn't tell exactly where it had originated. There were hundreds of people moving in all directions. Some of them got in line for the princess meet-and-greet on the other side of the strollers. Some headed to or from Toontown or the train station. Across the way was the busy entrance to the Fantasyland Theatre. Some guests joined the long queue for It's a Small World. There was a pile-up of people around the stroller area. The familiar scent vanished as quickly as it had come and Wolf was none the wiser.

Lance was startled when Wolf suddenly appeared next to him. "I thought you were over there."

With his back to the rest of the group, Wolf kept his voice low so only his security partner could hear him. "She was here."

Immediately tense, Lance's eyes started to scan the ever-changing myriad of guests. "Where?"

Wolf just shook his head and looked ready to punch something.

"I thought Steve was posted by the old dock. How'd she get past him?"

"There are other ways into the Park."

Lance had to concede and tried to relax before the kid's noticed something was wrong. He didn't want Catie to become fearful again. "True. That's just the only place we've actually seen her disappear. Don't worry. We'll get her eventually." Lance put a calming hand on Wolf's arm, mainly because he knew Wolf didn't like being touched.

"Yes, I will."

"**O**kay, you two ready for this? You have the screwdriver in your backpack, Peter?" Adam looked at the anxious, excited faces of Peter and Catie. He envied what they were about to do, remembering his own adventures and the adrenaline rush that came with it. "Lance, Kimberly, you have something figured out for a diversion?"

Kimberly's eyes narrowed when Lance gave her shoulders a tight squeeze. She wasn't sure she liked the grin that spread across his face. "Lance, what have you got planned?"

"You'll love it. Just play along."

"Lance...."

"Okay, then, we're all set." One thing Adam didn't envy was whatever Lance was about to do to Kimberly. He had been on the receiving end of those 'diversions' way too many times. "Beth, do you have something ready to drop into the water? Whatever it is you have to be totally upset about it."

Beth held out her hand, an innocent smile on her face. "Honey, could I use your phone for a minute."

As his hand dropped into his pocket, Adam noticed the mischievous glint in her eyes. "Hey, use your own phone! I need mine for work!"

"Just kidding. I have something else to use." Beth gave a light laugh as she watched Lance and Kimberly climb into the front row of the next boat. Her smile froze as Peter and Catie got into the back row. Heart pounding, she tried to tell herself that everything would be fine. The worse thing that could happen would be the kids getting caught and taken to Security. *But then*, she reasoned, *Wolf would be there, so that wouldn't be so bad*. She shook her head to concentrate on what she needed to do as the first boat began its slow journey toward the entrance of the ride.

Peter and Catie, along with everyone else in the general vicinity, looked back when Beth suddenly let out a loud shriek. Picked up by the gentle current, she frantically waved her arms and pointed at her water bottle already bobbing in front of the boat.

Adam called out that he would get it and hopped out of the boat—much to the dismay of the ride operators. Their closely-followed rules and time schedules were being broken right and left and they needed to get Adam back in the boat.

"Sir? You need to get back in the boat. We'll get it for you. No, don't get in the water! Don't…. Oh gosh! Sir?"

Adam took his time to reach the water bottle and then held it up in the air as if he had accomplished a daring feat of bravery. "Got it! Don't worry, honey, it's fine." He sloshed back through the water, slowly pulled himself up on the dock, and climbed back into the boat as if nothing odd had just happened.

Frustrated and not sure what to do, the ride operator hurriedly signaled the control tower to let the boat go. Adam gave an oblivious happy wave and shouted, "Thanks!" as their boat entered the channel, ignoring the surly looks from the cast members. Some of the people in line were laughing as they lowered their cameras and phones. You never knew what some crazy guest would do.

"Hope that next clue is worth ruining my shoes." Adam had his arm across the back of the rail behind Beth. Water pooled at his feet as it ran off of his soaked pant legs.

Once their boat had gotten underway, Beth had to control her giggles. "You should have seen your face! You looked so proud of yourself for rescuing my water bottle! Those cast members wanted to kill you." Her mirth sobered as she looked at the empty ride flume in front of them. "Do you think we gave the kids enough time?"

Adam gave a slight shrug and sighed. "Hope so. The only way it could have taken any longer was if I had swum a few laps."

"You'll have to remember that one for next time!"

"Next time? Yeah, next time."

Unaware of what had transpired at the loading dock, the ones in the first boat only knew it must have been successful. After repeatedly checking, they saw they had a clear channel behind them. With that knowledge came a slight lessening of tension. Adam had apparently put on a good enough performance and, now that the South Seas scene was just around the next bend, Lance had to do his job.

"Ouch!" Kimberly gave a startled yelp when Lance pinched her in the bottom. She sprang to her feet and immediately had to put her hands out to steady the rocking boat.

Lance stood next to her and tried to give her an awkward hug. "Now, come on, baby. Don't be like that. How about a little kiss?"

As desired, all heads in the boat turned to watch the drama in the front row. Peter nudged Catie and motioned for her to jump. The boat was only inches from the wide edge of the flume and was already rocking side to side. Nobody would notice. That had been Peter's fear that his and Catie's movements would make the boat dip to the side. Now his dad had arranged for that to be covered over.

"Get your hands off me, you cad!" Kimberly saw movement out of the corner of her eyes and

get caught, I want him to be the security guard who goes inside to get them."

"They haven't stopped the ride, so they must be handling it from behind the scenes."

After alerting Wolf, Lance led them to the shade of the gift shop—right where Omah had stood earlier. Unseeing of all that went on around them, the four adults merely stared at the glittering white and gold building. "I guess all we can do is wait. This is where the kids are supposed to meet us."

"I hate waiting."

Three heads slowly nodded in unison to Adam's mumbled words.

CHAPTER 11

Crouched down, Peter and Catie sprinted down the narrow space between the ride flume and the raised platform. They found a gap between the black entry wall of the South Seas room and the set where Peter could pull himself up. On his stomach, he helped Catie with the climb. Once in place, they ran behind the multi-layered walls of seaweed and the walls painted to resemble being underwater. As far back as they were they wouldn't be seen by a passing boat. The coral near the mermaids was tall enough to conceal them. They took a moment to catch their breath as they huddled in the darkness behind the set. Other than the singing and the clicks and whirrs of the mechanics around them, they could hear no other sound.

"We did it, Catie! I don't think anyone saw us."

The news of their success did nothing to relieve the pounding of her heart. Ever cautious, she peeked around the nearest corner to see if the next boats had caught up to them. "How long do you think we have?"

With the stealth of a Ninja, Peter crawled

around a stand of pink seaweed and slithered over behind the first mermaid. "I don't know. But we still need to hurry."

With one last, fearful glance at the empty ride flume, Catie joined her partner-in-crime. "It's so dark back there. Do you think there's a big backdrop to keep out the light like we found in the Haunted Mansion?"

Intent on finding the next capsule, Peter barely heard her whispered words. "Hmm? What? Oh, yeah, probably. That's how the cast members can work without being seen. I just wish I could have found the layout of this ride to show exactly where the outside exits are."

Eyes wide, Catie gave a gasp. "I thought you knew where everything was!"

Oops. He instantly realized he probably shouldn't have shared that last bit of information. "Oh, umm, I *think* I know. But the satellite map I was looking at wouldn't zoom in close enough." He glanced over and saw that her face had gone white—noticeable even in the shimmering blue that played over them. "Its okay, Catie, really. Just help me find the capsule so we can get out of here." He turned back to run his hand over all the seaweed trying to find anything that felt like it didn't belong.

She merely nodded and began to copy Peter's movements. "Should we just concentrate on the golden mermaid or should we try the others, too?"

Peter gave a shrug. "Well, according to the clue, I think just this one."

"Was she always in this spot?" She blushed when Peter turned to stare at her and felt she had to defend her question. "I...I was just wondering if we were looking in the right place. You know how things change. Ariel didn't use to be in here at all."

"No, no, you're right." Peter gave a quick glance at the ride flume when he thought he heard voices. He just couldn't tell if the sounds were from the next boat or from cast members. "I forgot all about that. This mermaid used to be on top, in Ariel's place. She had a crown on her head, if I remember the picture right. Good work, Catie!"

Her pleasure at his words was short-lived. "I think I hear someone talking, Peter. I don't think it's coming from a boat. It's back there."

"Yeah, I heard it, too. Hurry up."

"But, what if the clue's up at the top where Ariel is? How will we get up there without being seen?"

Peter glanced up at Ariel sitting in her mother-of-pearl shell, a smile on her face as she waved at the passing boats. The shell was held between two tall set pieces, one painted in muted greens and the other in subtle shades of blue. A tall piece of blue seaweed was off to one side of the shell as the scalloped bottom sat atop a pink piece, all covered with shimmering glitter. "Catie, you take the blue seaweed and I'll work on the pink one."

Both of the kids moved as fast as they could. The sounds they heard were getting closer—and they were coming from backstage. Anxious and frustrated, Catie was about to give up. "I don't see anything, Peter. I...wait, what's this?"

"You found something?" Peter stood from his hidden position and went over to Catie. Her hand was positioned on what looked like a board set crossways on the back of the set piece. There were no other boards like it that they could see. He gave a tentative tug, but it held firm as the tall seaweed swayed a little. "I think you're right. Get me that little gold screwdriver out of the top pocket. Hurry, Catie. Those voices are getting louder. I think they may be looking for us."

"Hurry, Peter! I don't want to get caught."

Peter grunted as he worked on the small brass screws that held the board in place. "Gosh, it's really stuck."

"I think I see a flashlight moving around over there! There has to be a boat coming, too. It's been way too much time. We've got to get out of here!"

"Your mom and dad should be in the front row."

"I don't care! Hurry!"

Peter had managed to pry the board a little ways away from the backing. Ignoring the two screws, he tugged with all his might and the board finally tore off the set.

"There they are!"

Both kids looked over to their right as two cast members came into view and shouted at them. "Back here, Catie! Jump off the platform and head toward that exit we saw at that wall of silver threads!"

"Okay, but that's where the next boat is coming from."

Adam and Beth had a mere glimpse of the two kids as they ducked into the emergency exit door. The brilliant white interior slowly faded to black as the door automatically shut and clicked. As they turned their attention back to the ride, they saw the seaweed next to Ariel still tottered back and forth.

"They're on the run." Beth had a tight grip on Adam's arm when she spotted the bobbing beams of two flashlights behind the set. That was enough to tell her that the kids had been spotted and were being chased. It took all she had not to jump out of the boat and run to help.

Even though he felt the same as his wife, Adam patted her hand and tried to pry her fingers from their death grip on his arm. "It'll be all right, honey. That's what happened to me in the big tunnel between New Orleans Square and Critter Country after I rappelled into the little blue cavern. I was spotted by the engineer of the train that was bearing down on me."

Beth allowed herself to be distracted and leaned into him. "What did you do? I hadn't joined the quest at that point."

"Ran like…uhm…as fast as I could. Ended up rolling down the stairs next to Splash Mountain." He shook his head and had to laugh at the sight he must have presented to the people waiting in line as he fell into them. "The kids are smart. And, Wolf is back there…somewhere…to help."

"I want to…."

"I know. I do, too, but we can't do anything right now. Look, we're almost outside already."

"I have my employee I.D. with me, Adam. Maybe I can…."

"Honey, let's just go tell Lance and Kimberly what we saw and wait—like we're supposed to."

"Grrr."

"I agree completely."

"There they are! Stop! You two kids, stop right now!"

Peter grabbed Catie's hand and ran around the tall black walls that hid the backstage area from the riders' eyes. They jumped over various cables and wires as they sought out the glowing red letters that spelled Exit. "There has to be an outside door close by. There wouldn't be so many emergency exits inside the ride if there wasn't one. It goes out onto a road or something outside."

"They're getting closer, Peter."

"I know. Look! There it is. There's the exit! Finally. Come on, Catie! Faster!"

The two kids burst out of the exit door, chests heaving from a mixture of excitement and nerves. Expecting to find Wolf, they looked around in dismay. As Peter had expected, they were on a roadway between the show buildings of Small World and Roger Rabbit. But, as Peter had not expected, it was empty.

"Where's Wolf?"

"I don't know, Catie. But we can't stand around here waiting for him. Those cast members should be coming out that door any minute now."

Catie looked in every direction. All she could see were buildings and cars and trees. "Where do we go? Where do we go?"

Peter made an instant decision and pointed. "Over there are the trees between Fantasyland and Toontown. We have to go that way to find our parents."

"Is there a door or does the road keep going?"

"I don't know. Just run!"

They headed south down the roadway, down the length of the building that housed Roger Rabbit's Car Toon Spin Ride.

"What are these tracks for? The train doesn't come this way at night, does it?"

At Catie's panted question, Peter glanced down at their feet as they ran. "No, it can't be the steam train. The tracks are too narrow. And, besides, the train's roundhouse is in the other direction."

Both kids could see that they were quickly running out of road and no obvious way out. Relief came when Peter pointed with his free hand. "There're two doors! Go in through the small one."

Just as the door to the Small World building burst open, the two kids disappeared into the doorway Peter had indicated. Flashlights in hand, the two cast members looked both ways on the empty road. Not knowing which way the kids had gone, they radioed their supervisor that they couldn't find the two children and inquired what should be done. After giving the descriptions of what they thought the kids were wearing, they went back into the show building.

"Oh, wow! Look through that window, Catie!"

"Peter, we need to get out of here! We don't belong here either. What is it?" Her curiosity got the better of her and she came back to Peter's side. "Hey, that's a Jolly Trolley. This must be where they keep them at night."

"That would explain the tracks outside, too. If they need repairs or something, there must be a machine shop back the other way."

Catie tugged on his arm. "Come on, Peter. This has to be a cast member only area. We need to go!"

Cautiously they opened the door and peered out. They found themselves next to the colorful entrance of Roger Rabbit. The large fountain was just across from them. Holding a broken steering wheel, Roger Rabbit himself posed on top of a gushing fire hydrant, water coming out of his ears. There was a long line of guests who circled the fountain as they waited to ride. "Act like you know what you're doing, Catie. Act casual."

Whistling, the two fugitives slowly strolled through the crowd and headed for the entrance/exit of Toontown that went under the railroad tracks and up into Fantasyland. A feeling of paranoia swept over both of them as they imagined everyone who passed by was looking for them.

Still walking slowly, Peter whispered to Catie, "Take off your jacket. Since we were spotted, they know what we're wearing. I'll take mine off, too. Now stuff them in my backpack. Too bad we don't have hats."

"We're almost at the toy shop. Mom and Dad should be there waiting for us."

They froze when four security guards led by Wolf suddenly came charging down the walkway. Eyes wide, they held their breaths as the three men and one woman got closer and closer. In the front position, with a subtle arm movement, Wolf signaled for them to get out of there. They released their breath in a relieved *Whoosh* as the guards passed them and headed into Toontown, turning right at the top of the hill.

Peter let out a loud laugh tinged with shaky relief. "Ha! Wolf to the rescue!"

Catie pulled on his arm to get him moving again. "Let's get to Mom and Dad. I don't want to be standing here when they come back."

Without a word, they broke into a run and quickly covered the remaining distance to where it all started—the front of It's a Small World.

Yorba Linda

At the insistent ringing of the doorbell, Margaret left the kids at the pool. She gave a firm warning for the two older boys to watch over Andrew while she answered the door.

Irritated that the bell continued to ring over and over, she flung open the door. The frown on her face was changed to a look of confusion. The photographs from her days as a mermaid still fresh in her mind, she couldn't grasp what she was seeing right in front of her. Her mouth opened and then closed again as she hung onto the doorframe with her free hand.

"Omah?" Her voice was barely a whisper. "Is that you?" Her brain warred with her eyes. So many years had passed, but this woman was young and beautiful. "It…it can't be you." Margaret shook her head as if the woman would somehow morph into the kind of face she saw in her mirror every morning. There must be another explanation. "No, you must be her daughter. Right?"

The woman in front of her gave her a slow head-to-toe scrutiny. A sarcastic half-smile came to her face—one that Margaret remembered all too well. It was a smile that showed Omah was feeling superior.

When her guest remained silent, Margaret pushed a strand of hair out of her eyes. She suddenly felt dowdy, unkempt in the face of this unlined face. "It is you, isn't it?" There was a sudden urge to go put on some makeup and fresh clothes.

"Hello, Margaret. It's been a long time." Once

again the piercing blue eyes gave Margaret the once-over. "A long, long time, apparently."

"I don't understand. How can you still be so…so…."

"Young? Fresh?"

"Er, yes, if you will."

Omah lifted one shoulder. "I had some work done."

A lot of work, Margaret added to herself, resist-ing the urge to smooth her blouse that the boys had splashed from the pool. *The boys*…. Margaret was torn. She felt she had to invite Omah in, but really didn't want to. The woman gave off a vibe that was unfriendly, somehow unsettling. With a vague point toward the back of the house, Margaret mentioned the boys were swimming in the pool.

She was saved the decision of closing the door or not when Omah invited herself in. "They must be your grandsons? How charming. Grandkids." There was a slight shiver that showed Omah felt children were anything but charming. "I'd love to meet them. Haven't seen John in ages, either." Omah was looking around the entry hall as if she was appraising the furniture. Her head suddenly swung back to Margaret. "Is he here?"

John had left an hour ago for a round of golf and wouldn't be home for a couple of hours. Mar-garet instantly felt she didn't want to share that knowledge. She hated to lie, but something didn't feel *right* with this woman. She managed to put a bright smile on her face as she led Omah out to the pool. "Oh, he's running some errands. I'm sure he'll be back before we know it."

"Lovely." Omah had been watching the house for about two hours. The golf clubs in the back of

John's pickup had told her a different story. "And you're still together. I remember how hard you fell for him. You didn't have eyes for anyone else after you met John."

After seeing that the boys hadn't drowned each other and were still content playing Marco Polo, she turned back to her guest. "So, tell me about yourself, Omah. Are you married? What have you been up to all these years?"

Omah waved off her question with a manicured hand. "Oh, here and there. I was sent to Florida after my mermaid stint ended." She had to clear her throat. Even she could hear the resentment, the bitterness tingeing her words. "But, enough of me. So, are all these boys yours? Aren't you going to introduce us?"

Margaret didn't like the way Omah's eyes darted from one boy to the next. Her protectiveness sprung into action. Taking the intruder by her arm, Margaret led her back into the living room and motioned for Omah to have a seat. "Oh, I don't want to disturb the boys right now. They're having so much fun. Who wants to talk to two old ladies?" She was surprised by the smug feeling she got at seeing Omah flinch at the word 'old.' "Now, tell me, Omah, what brings you here after all these years?" She tried to keep her voice light, but her smile was obviously forced.

Omah ignored the sofa and, instead, walked over to the bookcase lining the walls. Family pictures were interspersed with books and knick-knacks. She picked up a recent photo of Catie and appeared to study it. "Now, who is this lovely young girl? She has your look, Margaret, especially around the eyes."

been returned to its rightful spot?"

Margaret didn't like the fact that Omah stared at Catie again. Catie had found the capsule buried in the attic and the children had opened it to find another poem. She knew the two families were at Disneyland right now following up on yet another clue in what they jokingly called a treasure hunt. With a sinking feeling Margaret came to realize that somehow Omah knew all this. It felt like Oman was just baiting her. "What do you really want, Omah? It was just a silly poem buried in the Lagoon. Probably one of the submarine captains put it there. I always suspected Timothy. He was always doing silly stuff like that to us."

"No, it wasn't Timothy." Omah turned back and folded her arms, mimicking Margaret's defensive stance. "And I'm not interested in the clue and whatever was in that capsule. I just want the mermaid. That's all."

A look of confusion swept across Margaret's face. "Mermaid? What mermaid? The one from the Lagoon? It was stolen!"

"Yes, the mermaid from the Lagoon," she snapped, her hands balled into fists. All the chatty friendliness Omah had been pretending vanished in one nervous tic of the eye. She took a step closer to Margaret. "You have no idea what that mermaid means or how long I have searched for it. I will have it!"

Did she just stamp her foot? Margaret held herself back from glancing at the backyard and kept eye contact with the oddly-acting woman in front of her. She didn't want to draw attention to the boys. By the sounds she could hear, she knew they were now playing on the swing set and were safe. Something was wrong with this woman from her past— more than just the annoying, superior attitude she had been subjected to almost fifty years ago. Margaret kept her voice low and reasonable. "Now, I don't have that mermaid, Omah. You know it was stolen. You know I came back empty-handed. How could I possibly have the mermaid?"

"I know you don't have it." The words came out fast and bitter. "I'm not as stupid as everyone assumes." She made an effort to calm herself, but it didn't work. "You might not have it, but I think you know who does." She spun back to the shelf and grabbed Catie's picture to thrust it into Margaret's hands. "Little Catie knows who has it, too. Do you want *me* to ask her? I'd be more than happy to oblige."

Margaret clutched the picture protectively to her chest. "You leave Catie out of this. You'll have to go through me to get to her."

The sneering smile was back. "And, yet, here I am. Catie and Peter know exactly where my mermaid is."

"Peter! How do you know Peter?" This was too much for Margaret. The knuckles that hung onto Catie's photograph were white. "I want you out of my house. Don't you ever come near Catie or Peter or me again. I don't want you to even speak their names. Do you hear me?"

"Or what?"

"Do not come between a mother bear and her cubs." Margaret firmly set the picture on the table next to her and pointed to the front of the house. "You'll not be told again."

A low chuckle came from Omah. "I'll go, but this isn't over. I'll even be reasonable about it. I'll give you three days to get my mermaid and have it here at this…lovely…house. Or you might just see how well a mother bear does against a wolf."

"Out."

Her next words chilled Margaret to the core. "So, do you think they're done at Disneyland yet? Have a magical day. Three of them, to be exact." With an eerie laugh she headed to the old car that was parked across the street. Dented and abused, it belched a cloud of black smoke as it pulled away from the curb.

Margaret watched until Omah turned the corner and was out of sight. The front door was slammed, locked and bolted. Breathing hard, Margaret leaned back against the secured door and closed her eyes. She had never before been around anyone who was insane and wasn't sure if that appellation applied to Omah. "I've never seen that look in anyone's eyes before and I sure don't want to see it again. What happened to you, Omah?"

Hearing the boys calling her, Margaret realized she was shaking and muttering to herself. "They can't see me this way. Mother Bear needs to relax." With a shake of her head, she headed to the back of the house to attend to the needs of her cubs. *That woman won't lay a hand on them while I'm around.*

CHAPTER 12

Disneyland

Now that the mission had been deemed a success and the odd-shaped board was hidden away in Peter's backpack, the two kids were able to relax. Their playfulness came back when they passed the Tomorrowland Terrace. The Jedi Training Academy was in full swing as young Jedi guests engaged in a mock battle with Darth Vader and his Stormtroopers.

Peter and Catie pulled imaginary lightsabers from their sides and started their own fight with all the requisite sound effects. Attempting a full spin, Peter tripped over an oncoming baby stroller and sprawled on the ground. Catie proclaimed herself the victor as Peter got to his feet.

Instead of conceding gracefully, his empty hand slowly passed in front of her face. He somehow managed to keep his face straight and his voice calm as he intently stared at her. "These are not the droids you are looking for."

Playing along, Catie let her expression go slack. "These are not the droids I am looking for."

"Move along."

"I will move along."

"Have a nice day."

"Have a…. Don't push it, Peter."

"Dad, can we go on Star Tours?"

Lance gave a laugh as he turned to the other parents and lifted his left hand. "Okay, show of hands. Who saw that one coming?"

As the discussion turned to the necessity of FastPasses for the popular ride, Adam's cell phone rang. He glanced at the caller I.D. "It's my mom. Hope the boys haven't worn her to a frazzle. Hey, Mom, how's everything?"

Lance turned around when Adam suddenly hit him in the arm to get his attention. The sarcastic comment ready on his lips died when he saw the serious look on Adam's face. "What's up? Something wrong with the boys?"

Adam just shook his head and kept listening, a frown on his face. "Is Omah still there? Where's Dad? Oh, that's right…. What do you mean? How did she threaten you? What did she say exactly?"

While Adam kept his mother on the line, Lance pulled out his two-way radio and called for Wolf to join them. He knew the security guard would still be in Fantasyland to deal with the break-in on Small World. Wolf had to go through the standard procedures until enough time had passed and everyone felt everything had been done to code. Since the two children had gotten away and apparently nothing was damaged, the matter would soon drop.

"This is getting more serious, Lance." Kimberly and Beth confronted Lance while the two kids were still busy at the FastPass machine. "How did that woman even know where Margaret lived? It was my impression that they hadn't even spoken since their mermaid days. And now she is threatening Margaret? Why?"

Adam put away his phone and ran a nervous hand through his hair. "I don't know. Mom said that Omah only wanted the mermaid the kids found in the Mansion. She gave Mom three days to have it at the house."

"Or what?" Wolf had just joined them, his face angry and determined.

Adam could only shrug. "According to Mom, Omah didn't say what she would do. Just gave her the ultimatum."

"We need to get to Yorba Linda, Adam. Now."

Peter and Catie arrived just in time to hear that they were leaving Disneyland. "Awww! We just got FastPasses!"

Lance put an understanding hand on his son's shoulder. "Sorry, buddy, but we have to go. That Omah woman was just at Grandma Margaret's house. We need to make sure she's okay."

Catie's eyes got wide as Peter clamped his mouth shut. Star Tours would have to wait for another day. Family was more important.

"I'll meet you there. I have to check out of work first." Wolf turned to go but was stopped by Peter's next words.

"Can I ride with Uncle Wolf?" Always ready to jump on any silver lining in his clouds, Peter was quick on the draw.

Lance turned to Kimberly and silently asked her opinion. She raised one shoulder in a slight gesture. "I suppose it would be all right. There isn't

think he was emoting *exactly* what he was thinking. I shudder to think what it would be like if he had formal training. Now, let's get down to business." He shot a brief look at the kitchen door. It wasn't too far a stretch to imagine Peter on the other side listening. With a lowered voice he continued. "Even though I know this won't go over well, I think we should open the next clue and see where this is leading. Then we'll talk about that mermaid."

"Don't you think Peter and Catie should at least be in on the opening?"

Lance looked up from digging through Peter's messy backpack. "Gosh, how does he find anything in here…. I know, Kimberly, but this is getting to be way over their heads. We don't always get what we want." He finally pulled out the board that Peter had yanked off the Small World set.

Adam came over when he saw the glitter-covered item. "Hey! That looks a lot like the two-by-four we found in Walt's first garage studio in Kansas City. Remember, Lance? It was up in the rafters and had been painted to blend in perfectly with its surroundings." He took the light blue piece of wood from Lance's hands and turned it over. "If Walt had it made the same way, there should be a secret opening back here. A little sliding door or something." He stopped and looked at his fingers that were now covered with sparkling blue glitter. "Great. I look like Catie's school binder…."

"Are you going to reminisce forever or are you going to open it?"

At Lance's impatient remark, Margaret, Beth and Kimberly rolled their eyes at each other. *Boys.*

"Gosh, give me a minute. Wow, to think this has been hanging there since the 1960's. Walt sure knew what he was doing. Hiding in plain sight. Just like...."

"Open it."

All eyes turned to the usually silent Wolf after his terse two-word command. They knew he was taking the appearances and vanishings of Omah personally.

"Yes, boss." Adam took a small folding knife out of his pocket and ran it under a barely-notice-able notch.

"You went to Disneyland armed? Planning on defending the Castle with that tiny thing?"

Hearing the amusement in Lance's voice, Adam glanced up. "Tiny but deadly in the hands of an expert."

"Too bad we didn't bring an ex...."

"Will you two knock it off and open it?"

"Yes, dear." Adam glanced up and his smile faded a little. "Oh, sorry, Kimberly. You sounded just like...."

"Open it!"

"Hey, you all don't have to gang up on me at once! Sheesh. Remember, I am armed." He held up the one-inch blade and received a unanimous round of indifference. "Fine. I'll open it. Wow, this is really jammed in there."

All five of the adults in the room leaned forward as the blade of the knife lifted a small, fitted panel off the back of the wooden board. The first thing to fall out was a ring and it immediately fell to the carpet.

Seated next to her son, Margaret leaned over and scooped up the golden object. "Why, that's a claddagh ring! How beautiful! Oh, look at the tiny diamonds circling the heart."

Always up on his Disney trivia, Adam stopped trying to pull a couple pieces of paper out of the small opening. "A claddagh ring? Really? That's what Walt and Lillian both wore. You can see Walt's on his right hand if you look at the Partner's Statue at Disneyland." He looked around at the faces that stared at him and gave a sigh. "Fine, I'll finish what I'm doing."

"While we're still alive to appreciate it." They all heard Lance's muttered remark—as he had intended.

The painted two-by-four had been hollowed out and smoothed on the inside. Various coats of paint and glitter had protected it against detection. Adam still marveled—silently—that it had remained unfound for over forty years. The Small World attraction had been built for the New York World's Fair in 1964 and was moved to Disneyland after the Fair closed in 1965. It opened to the public in May of 1966. As he carefully finagled the paper stuck inside so it didn't rip, he kept his facts to himself. "Got it. It looks like another page out of the diary. And this is some kind of brochure." He handed the colorful artwork to his wife as he eagerly read the handwritten note. When he was done he looked up at his family and friends who were expecting to be told what he had silently read to himself. Lips dry, he saw that they were impatient and would turn on him at a moment's notice. "Uhm, this is unexpected. Beth, let me see the front of that brochure." When she held it and he saw the artwork, he grimaced. "I don't know if it is good news or bad."

Flashback — Disneyland — 1965

Walt glanced at his visitor who had finally quit his persistent pacing. The blonde-haired man now stood motionless as he stared out of Walt's apartment window that overlooked Main Street. Walt set his pen down and rubbed his tired eyes. "You nervous or something?"

His right-hand man didn't turn from his place as he watched the Fire Engine slow to a stop in front of City Hall. "What? Oh, no. Just thinking."

"Anything deep and thought-provoking?"

There was a light laugh. "Oh, I don't know about that. Maybe. I was just thinking about the future. Where I'll be and all that."

At the mention of the future, Walt startled a little and his hand moved to cover what he had been writing. He hadn't shared this particular venture with his friend yet, only one other person. After tapping his index finger on the piece of paper, he gave a mental shrug. *Why not? It might be good to have a second opinion.* "Maybe you could take a look at something I've been working on and tell me what you think."

"You writing a story, Walt?" As the man turned to face his boss, a smile crossed his face.

"Well, I am a storyteller. Of all the things I've ever done, I'd like to be remembered as a storyteller."

The smile broadened. "I think that's a safe thing to want. You're known around the whole world as a storyteller."

Walt's expression turned thoughtful. "Yeah, I

guess you're right, but will it last?" He glanced down at the table in front of him. "That's kinda what I'm working on now. You know that girl Omah from the Lagoon?"

Tall. Shapely. Red hair. Dark, almost exotic features. "Yeah, she's one of the mermaids."

There was a pause before Walt responded. "Yeah, she's a mermaid. Too." At the confused look on his friend's face, Walt continued. "I haven't told you about her yet, but she works for me, too. Besides being a mermaid, I mean."

"Works doing what?"

"Well, kinda like you, only not so much." Walt stood from the table and rubbed a hand across the back of his neck. Stiff from a polo injury, it was giving him trouble today. "I have an idea for a…well…I guess you could call it a treasure hunt I'm setting into place. I haven't bothered you with it because it doesn't amount to much. If things go well…." Walt broke off and gave a shrug. *Who knows with something like this? How long would it take to see if it worked or not?* He shrugged again and walked back to his chair. "Well, if I see the need, I'll come to you with something even bigger, more involved."

"I don't understand. What treasure hunt? What are you planning to hide?"

Walt looked down at the paper on which he had been writing. "Why don't you read this and I'll fill in the missing pieces of what I've already done when you're finished." Walt handed the sheet to the outstretched hand and then walked out onto the covered patio. Beneath the overhang was the walkway into the City Hall. Behind him he could hear the occasional shots from the Jungle Cruise skippers. But, he wasn't thinking about this jewel of a park. He, too, was thinking about the future.

"*Hi, there.*

I hope you have been enjoying the Mermaid's Tale. Didn't know there were so many mermaids in my little Park, did you? Or, if you've gotten this far, perhaps you did.

There is one more step in this Tale before you're finished. You might have heard me say that I don't like to repeat successes. I like to go on to other things. Well, you'll be going to a new place next and do something you probably have never done before. <u>Be careful!</u>

I hope you've been paying attention to where you've gone. Each place has been special to me and, I hope, loved by thousands of guests. Remember the fun you have had in each of these places and remember the old man who created them all for you! It's my sincerest hope that my legacy will continue long after I'm gone. This little quest you have been on is one way of seeing who is tenacious enough, strong enough to see it through. There is something special for you at the end. Use it as you will.

Mermaids have always been special to me. Some legends have them as dark and ugly. Mine, in my mind, have always been beautiful creatures. I have owned The Little Mermaid *since way back in 1941. I had even thought about doing a film right after* Snow White, *but there were problems—as there commonly are—and it was put on hold. When there were problems at the studio and then the wartime efforts, another project featuring* The Little Mermaid *was shelved in 1943. Even after all this time, I still haven't gotten around to it. But, it is always in the back of my mind. I see her with red hair,*

They bypassed the Castle and walked between the Matterhorn Mountain and the Alice in Wonderland ride. The Storybook Land Canal Boats had a large line of guests as did Autopia and the Motor Boat Cruise. As they neared the back end of the Park, Walt stopped for a minute to look at his latest masterpiece that could be partially seen over the blockade of construction walls. The white façade of It's a Small World was incomplete, but one could still see the whimsical, worldwide appeal of the building.

There was no water in the unfinished canal and there were a few walkways over it. Walt nodded hello to various workers who stopped to gape at their boss. Even though they saw him often as he checked on the progress, it was still a surprise to see him walk through the clutter and debris. Always inconspicuous, his companion was unnoticed as he trailed behind Walt.

Keeping to the west side of the building, Walt led him unerringly to the South Seas display. The dolls were not in place yet, but the backgrounds for most of the scenes were in position. Plain blue, wavy pieces of wood stood upright in a cluster. "This is where the three mermaids will be." Walt pointed upwards. "The queen mermaid will be up there. There'll be a couple of turtles hovering up near her, too. Well, you remember what it looked like in New York." Walt walked behind the un-adorned set. "Let me have the screwdriver and screws. This one will go right here."

As Walt happily got to work setting the new piece of wood, his companion had a question. "How do you know it won't be moved?"

Humming the Small World theme song, Walt

gave a short chuckle. "It won't be moved. These pieces are here to stay. And, once it gets a spraying of glitter, it won't even be seen."

"You're pretty sure of yourself, Walt."

Arms folded, Walt stood back to admire his handiwork. "Yeah, I am. A lot of people...a LOT of people said Disneyland would be closed and forgotten after the first year. And here we are ten years later. I'm sure. Come on. Your job is next."

Five minutes later, Walt and the blonde-haired man stood in a different part of Fantasyland. Every few moments, a Skyway bucket would cast a quick shadow over the two men. The screams and laughter coming from the spinning Tea Cup ride behind them were unheard as one man looked confident, almost smug, and the other man looked confused.

"Where am I supposed to be looking?"

Walt patted the pocket of his cardigan. "Remember the brochure that went into this gray capsule?"

The man's eyes widened. "Yes." The word was drawn out so long that it sounded like two syllables.

A big smile on his face, Walt looked upward and pointed. His friend went pale. "It goes right there."

"Wow, other than being folded to fit inside the wooden beam, the brochure is in perfect condition. Does it say what year it was printed?"

At Lance's question, Beth turned over the bright ad for the restaurant. "No, but I read somewhere that the pirate ship had been in Disneyland from 1955 to around 1982. They added Skull Rock and some beautiful waterfalls in 1960, if I remember right." She held up the paper. "This could have been printed at any point during that time."

Adam interrupted any further discussion of the brochure. "All that is fine and good, but it looks to me as if our problem with the kids continuing this treasure hunt has just solved itself."

"What do you mean, honey?"

Adam looked at Beth as if he couldn't understand how she could not see this. "This ship no longer exists. Whatever Walt had in mind is now gone. The hunt has now ended. Too early for the kids sake, but it is effectively over." Expecting agreement from all the adults in the room, he had to frown when Lance, Kimberly and Wolf put their heads together in an obviously private discussion. "Something you'd like to share with the class, guys?"

Margaret had taken the brochure from Beth and was fondly reminiscing about one of the more beautiful spots in Fantasyland. "We used to enjoy having lunch there. The tuna salad was served in these little pirate ship bowls. We'd take our food over this wooden bridge and sit under awnings that looked like sails from the ship." She set the folded paper in her lap and smiled as she continued. "The tables were shaped like barrels, if I recall correctly. Do you remember any of that, Adam? You were young. I might have some pictures in one of our albums."

Adam pulled his mind from the kid's coming disappointment. "Kinda. Didn't we have to walk up this long wooden plank or walkway or something to get inside? There were stairs everywhere. I always wanted to climb the mast and check out the crow's nest."

"The lights inside and around Skull Rock always made that area look so lovely at night." Margaret gave a small sigh at the necessity of progress. "We were sorry when the ship was torn down. Some of the rides were moved around after that. Dumbo is in that spot now and the Tea Cups were moved over by Alice in Wonderland."

Adam used part of her last remark to bring the discussion back to the treasure hunt. "That's right. It was torn down. Other than some piece or other being put into the Peter Pan ride, it's gone. So, we need to break the news to the kids." He could see a small look of relief on Beth's face when she realized that Peter and Catie would no longer be in danger from Omah. But he could also tell that she was disappointed by this obvious end of their adventure. "So, how do we tell the kids?" Again he was stopped by the looks exchanged among the Brentwoods and Wolf. "What? I don't see any other outcome here. Do you?"

Lance took a deep breath and looked one more time at Wolf. He received a cautious nod from the security guard. "Hmmm. Well, yes, there is another option. It's one we didn't think we'd have to use."

"The Pirate Ship is gone, Lance. Unless you or Wolf know where the pieces were buried or stashed or…."

"There is another way. Can I see the brochure, please?" Lance took the ad and went into discussion with Wolf again. Lance pointed at one part of the ship but Wolf didn't seem to agree.

Wolf's finger stabbed lower and a slight smile crossed his lips. "Knowing Walt, I would think it would be here. That's the closest accessible spot to her fingers."

Adam shook his head and rubbed the bridge of his nose. "I'll get back to your 'knowing Walt' comment in a moment. But, you're still discussing this as if it will happen. The. Ship. Is. Torn. Down."

"Yes, Adam, we know that." Wolf spoke up and seemed to be choosing his words carefully. "Now, in our time, yes, the ship is gone. It's been gone for a couple of decades now. And, no, the part of the ship I'm leaning toward isn't what was used inside Peter Pan."

Thoroughly confused, Adam, Beth, and Margaret could only silently stare at Wolf. They could tell he was leading up to something, but had no idea what it might possibly be. There seemed to be a split in the room, a division, with Lance, Kimberly and Wolf on one side and Adam, Beth, and Margaret on the other. Only, Adam, Beth, and Margaret had no idea why there even *was* a division.

Wolf cleared his throat and looked uncomfortable. "It is possible to go back and retrieve the next clue that was hidden on the Pirate Ship."

Adam tried again. Keeping his voice calm, he sounded as if he was talking to someone very dense. "Yes, Wolf, we know we can go back to the Park. We were just there—and there is no Pirate

Ship in Fantasyland."

"No, that's not what I am saying. I mean we can go back to Disneyland when the Pirate Ship was still there and get the clue that I think is hidden somewhere in that crow's nest."

Adam looked at the serious look on Wolf's face and saw it mirrored on Lance's and Kimberly's. Expecting them to drop the joke at any moment, he got a wide smile on his face. "Oh, I didn't know you had a Delorean in your garage. I thought you drove a Mustang! Or, are you really Mr. Peabody and have a Way Back Machine stashed somewhere?" He laughed and turned to Beth to see her reaction to his witty remark.

However, Beth wasn't looking at Adam and she wasn't smiling along with him. Her eyes were wide, the same look that was on Margaret's face. Both women stared at Wolf. "You aren't kidding, are you, Wolf?"

At his shake of the head, she continued. "We've known you a long time, Wolf. You've always been straight with us. This all sounds really weird, but you don't joke around much, do you?" She didn't wait for any reply. Some pieces to a long-standing puzzle in her mind had started to drop into place. Her heart began to pound in her chest and her mouth had gone dry. When she continued, her voice dropped to a whisper. "You look the same as you did the day we first met you. And, I've seen the picture of you with Kimberly's father and Walt in Lance's office. You look the same age then as you do now."

"What are you saying, Beth, dear?" Margaret had gone a little pale. She had known Wolf almost as long as she had known Adam's best friend

Lance. There had been little things she had noticed over the years, too, but never thought too much about them.

Beth turned to her mother-in-law and patted her hand. "I actually don't know what I'm getting to, but I think there is more to our Wolf than we know." She faced their friend again. "Isn't that right, Wolf?"

Wolf came back from pacing the room. He was torn. It was vital that his secret remain hidden—as it had been for centuries. Only a select few knew about his strange ability: His family and village, Walt, Kimberly's father, Lance, Kimberly, Wals, Peter, Dr. Houser, and a few trouble-makers that had to be taken elsewhere. To keep a secret safe, he knew it was best that the fewer who knew it the better. "Yes." *How much do I say? How far do I have to go to explain myself?* "For many…years…I have had the…ability…to open portals to the past." He received the expected raised eyebrows and mouths that opened and then closed again. But, they remained silent to hear him out. "It's possible for me to open a portal to the past so we can re-trieve the clue. I've done it before and it's…well, it's a little exhausting for me, but it is safe. Only…." Again he paused. *This is the hard part.* "I have to take someone with me to do the actual retrieving of the clue."

"Let's just say that we," Adam began, indicating himself, Beth and Margaret, "believe you and this is possible. *If* this is possible." Adam ran a hand through his hair, a sign that he was confused and frustrated. "Why do you need someone else to go along? Couldn't you just get it yourself and open this…portal, did you call it?…and come back?"

If possible, Wolf looked even more uncomfortable. He would rather be anywhere else than having to explain to three people he cared about and could see they thought he was a little off in the head. "I'd rather not say. It's something that could *really* be misunderstood."

"That's an understatement." All of them could hear Lance's muttered comment.

Adam immediately turned on his friend. "You know what he's talking about? You've known about it for how many years and you never told me? After all we've been through together?"

Lance held his hands up in front of him. "Hey, don't shoot me."

Adam's head tilted to the side and his eyes narrowed. "That is so not funny. How do you know so much about it?"

"I've seen it. I've gone with him."

"What?" This time it was Kimberly who stepped into the conversation. "What are you talking about? I know what Wolf does, but what does it have to do with you?"

"Oops." Lance had forgotten Kimberly didn't have any memory of his and Peter's trip back with Wolf to fix the missing Haunted Mansion. They had arrived back in their own day an hour or so before Kimberly had known they were gone. It was as if they had never left in her eyes. "The point is that I'm fine and it does work. I don't know how he does it, but it is his reality."

"You really can travel through time." Margaret spoke up, her hand still tightly grasped in Beth's. "To any time you want?"

At Wolf's brief nod, she slightly shook her head side to side, a small smile coming over her face. "To be able to see those who are no longer with us.

full name is Sumanitu Taka. It means wolf. My brother is Mato which means bear."

"I thought your name was Mani Wolford."

"Mani is taken from Sumanitu."

"So your real name is Wolf Wolford...."

Wolf gave an irritated shake of his head. He had gone through this same conversation with Wals Davis years ago when he needed Wals assistance in the past. *Maybe I should have gone to Wals for help instead of going through this again....* His answer was almost a growl. "Yes, it is. Can we get back to the point?

"Is your brother really a bear, then?"

"No! Mato is not a bear!"

"So, you're a werewolf."

"No, Adam, I am not a werewolf!" Wolf had to stop for a minute and he rubbed a hand over his face. "Look, my mother was attacked when she was pregnant with me by a weird, talking wolf. My father tracked it down after she died and killed it. He wears the wolf's skin as a remembrance to my mother."

"Your father runs around town in a wolf skin?" This was getting more and more bizarre to Adam.

"He doesn't live in town, Adam. He...he only is alive back in time. I go back and visit when I can."

Margaret turned to Beth and grinned. "That sounds just like the Shaman in the Friendly Village on the Frontierland River." Their smiles froze when Wolf didn't deny the claim. "Oh, my. This is bigger than I thought."

Lance could see he needed to step in and help Wolf or they would be here all day. From the rambunctious sounds coming from the kitchen, he knew the boys and Catie had had just about all the alone time they needed. "Now that we have this all straight in our minds...." He held up a hand to stop the flood of comments that was sure to come. "Now we can get down to business and give Wolf a moment's peace. He is what he is and you all know his qualities. Such as they are..." he added in a loud undertone. "We just have to decide who will go with him to get the next clue. I volunteer myself as I have already been through it. We can just pop into Disneyland, I'll climb the mast you think it is hidden in, and we'll be home before anyone is the wiser."

Before anyone could say yes, no, or maybe, Wolf looked at Kimberly—who obviously wasn't pleased with Lance's words. Even though Lance said he had gone with Wolf, she had no memory of it and, so she was still somewhat frightened at this strange ability of Wolf's. *She won't like this suggestion, either.* "Kimberly, I was thinking that you and Peter should go with me, not Lance." Seeing that she was just about to negate that idea, he held up a hand. "Hear me out, please. Here is why I think you should go. I can't just pop into Disneyland as Lance suggested. Portals are...iffy. I could come out in the middle of Main Street. And, since I will be a wolf, I don't see that going over very well."

Lance jumped in before Kimberly could. "So, if you aren't going straight to Disneyland, where will you go?"

Wolf turned his eyes on his friend. "To your house."

"What will that accomplish? You'll be with us."

Wolf gave a slight shake of his head. "You're not thinking of the past. It'll be the same house, only...."

"My father will be there. Walt's right-hand

her face. "I hope you aren't in too much trouble. Is Wolf with you? I'd like to talk to him, too."

The boy shuffled his feet. "Umm, he is here, but he didn't think you'd recognize him if we didn't say something first."

There was a light laugh. "I just saw him at Disneyland yesterday. I think I'd recognize my good friend."

"Maybe not like this." Peter gave a sharp whistle. "Wolf! Here, boy!"

They all heard an unmistakable growl come from the side of the house. "I told you not to call me that way, Peter."

At the familiar voice, the man looked in the direction from which it had come. "You hiding for some reason, Wolf?"

"You might say that." Wolf cautiously emerged from the shadows. Ears alert and tail up, his familiar blue eyes stared back at his friend.

The blonde-haired man took an involuntary step back. "Wolf? Is that really you?" He came off the porch and went over to the huge animal. A hand lifted, but he paused. "I probably shouldn't pet you, should I?"

Wolf gave a light laugh. "Peter here does it every chance he gets. I'm getting used to it."

The man took a slow walk about the wolf. "So this is what happens. I've always wondered. You told me about it, but, it's not the same as seeing it." He suddenly stopped his rambling and had to clamp his open mouth shut.

"You just figured it out, didn't you?"

The man slowly nodded. "You only change into a wolf when you go back to the past." Walking back to the porch, he shakily sat down on the top step. "You'll forgive me if I take a moment. This is quite unusual. Well, for me, that is." He looked up at Kimberly and Peter who had remained silent through all this. "You're from the future, too? Who are you?"

Kimberly was about to answer, but looked to Wolf first. He gave a nod of his head. "It's okay. You won't affect the future in any way."

The tears returned to her green eyes. "Daddy! It's me, Kimberly. This is your grandson, Peter. There're two more boys, but they were too young to bring."

"Daddy?" The word was whispered as the man got slowly to his feet. He put out a tentative hand to touch the woman's face, but stopped just short of her cheek. "That's why you look so familiar. You look just like…the woman I'm dating." He gave a laugh and turned to the wolf. "I guess we're more serious than I realized!" His fascinated attention turned to the boy. "Peter, is it? Fine name." He glanced up knowingly at Kimberly. "Fine name! Thank you."

"Can I call you Grandpa?"

Peter's question stopped everyone in their tracks. What do they call each other? It was possible the man would be seen by friends. He, an unmarried man, couldn't introduce them as his daughter and grandson. Kimberly looked to be about the same age he was, maybe a little older—even though he knew better than to ask. Plus, it was known he was dating someone else, not this woman.

"Perhaps that wouldn't be best right now, Peter." He put a fond hand on the boy's light hair. "Let's just play it by ear. Why don't you all come in-parking is only twenty-five cents? Nice! Can I have that parking ticket?"

Kimberly looked at her father with a wide grin on her face. "I have a feeling its going to be a long day. He won't stop, you know."

An attendant waved the Lincoln into a two-car parking spot. Over in the next aisle, they saw a tram was winding through the lot to take new arrivals to the front gate. "Peter, that's the Mark II monorail. I hear we're going to get another train, a green one, pretty soon." He turned back to answer Kimberly. "I don't mind his chatter, honey. Oh, I guess I should call you Kimberly, shouldn't I? Sorry."

As they approached the tram Kimberly tucked his arm into hers. "You always called me honey. I…I like it."

He could hear the catch in her voice and again marveled at Wolf's ability to do this wonderful thing. How many people get a glimpse into their own future or their past? As they took a hard plastic seat on the tram, he just smiled as he watched his grandson. Peter was looking every which way trying to take it all in. There were unasked questions all over the boy's face. Wolf had cautioned all three of them to not ask or reveal anything about the future. However, just by listening to Peter, he had already learned a lot. He figured he would learn much more before they returned home to Fullerton later that evening.

"So, what day is this again? I know you told me, but it didn't sink in at the time."

The tram pulled to a stop right in front of the entrance gate. The steam train at the Main Street Station blew its whistle and started its trip around the Magic Kingdom.

"It's May 28th, 1966."

"Why does that date sound so familiar?"

Her father just shrugged. "It's a Small World is going to open to the public today. Would that be something that will be remembered?"

"That's it! Wow, it's brand new right now. The kids had to search.... Oh, never mind."

He gave her arm a squeeze and leaned closer for a conspiratorial whisper. "That's all right. I helped Walt set it in place."

"Mom! It's only four dollars and fifty cents for a whole ticket book! Can I buy an extra one for Catie? She doesn't have an original entry ticket."

"That would be nice, Peter. Do you have enough money?"

Peter pulled a beat-up wallet out of his back pocket. Kimberly saw her father doing the exact movement at the same time. They both looked up when she laughed. "Never mind." She waved them off, her hand over her mouth. They had the exact stance, as well.

Just before Peter could hand a twenty-dollar bill to the cast member in the booth, his grandfather snatched it from him. "Wait a minute, son. Let me see that." He gave a surprised look at Kimberly. "That's a lot of money for a child to carry around."

"It's my allowance!"

"Yeah, it's not so much…from where we come from." Kimberly had to amend her statement when other people were pressing closer around them.

"No, that's not why I grabbed it, Peter. It looks…different, that's all. Our money doesn't have color and so much printed on it. I just don't want questions to start if they think it's counterfeit. Here,

It just slipped out."

His grandfather looked like he needed to find a place to sit. *Perhaps the boy meant something else. Maybe Walt would be in Florida when the ride opened. Maybe that's what he left out.* He knew his boss had some health problems, but it was Walt… *Well, Walt would live forever, wouldn't he? No, I can't ask. I can't know something like that. Whatever comes will come. Kimberly was right. This is harder than we thought.* He turned to look back at Peter. The boy looked like he was ready to cry. Putting a kind hand on the boy's shoulder, he gave him a reassuring smile. "Don't fret, son. You didn't really tell me anything. So, let's just forget this and get ourselves to the Pirate Ship. I have a surprise for you."

The promise of something special immediately picked up Peter's spirits. "What is it? Will I like it? Where do we go?"

Kimberly leaned into her father. "That worked. Thanks."

"My pleasure. Well, Peter, if I told you, it wouldn't be a secret, would it?"

"Gosh, that's what Mom says all the time."

"Where do you think I learned it, Peter?" as she gave her father's arm another squeeze.

When they stepped through the Castle, Peter's eyes widened as he looked around. "There's Peter Pan, but look at the front of it! It's all…flat."

"Did you ever hear what Walt said about Fantasyland? 'What youngster has not dreamed of flying with Peter Pan over moonlit London, or tumbling into Alice's nonsensical Wonderland? In Fantasyland, these classic stories of everyone's youth have become realities for youngsters–of all ages–to participate in.' It was a proud day for all of us when that drawbridge lowered for the first time."

"Remember, Peter, Walt ran out of money and decided to go with a medieval tournament look for Fantasyland. What you're used to wasn't built until….uhm, later." Kimberly shot a quick glance at her father. "Gosh, Wolf is going to kill us for talking too much."

Their guide just smiled. He wasn't concerned about Wolf. "You know so much about…well, I guess it would be history for you. Current times for me. It warms my heart to know that the love of the Park has lived on through my family line. Don't worry about Wolf. I don't plan on telling him anything!"

"Me, either!" Kimberly pointed ahead for Peter. "See? The Skyway is working. Maybe we can ride that later. Oh, and there's Dumbo."

"Where's the water…."

"Pete."

"Well, this is hard! It's all so different, but it's still the same. It's kinda confusing."

"Yes, it is, Peter, but we're here to do a job. Don't forget that."

"Yes, Mom." At the mention of his upcoming task, Peter walked past the Tea Cups and a big smile came across his face. "Wow, that's really big!"

"Pictures don't do it justice." Kimberly came up behind him and put her hands on his shoulders. "The colors are so vivid and bright. And the sails are out. Will that make it harder for Peter…. Are you sure it's safe for him to climb up there?" The higher her eyes went, the more nervous she became.

Her father patted her hand. "It's all right, Kimberly. I did it. Not that long ago, either. He just has to go slow and steady."

"What's my surprise?"

"My, you don't forget anything, do you, my boy?"

Peter smiled up at his grandfather. "Nope. Dad says I'm like a sponge. Hey, there's the mermaid on the front of the ship! I'm hungry. Can we get lunch while we're here?"

As they walked across the plank walkway, Kimberly noticed something. "There's no one else in here. Did you shut down the area?"

The sharp green eyes, so like her own, turned on her. "Now, how did you know I could do that? Never mind. Don't tell me. In a word, yes, I did." He led them downstairs into the serving area. Brass lanterns hung from the low beamed ceiling and the menu was printed onto fish-shaped signs. "You can change down here, out of sight."

"Change into what?"

His grandfather's eyes sparkled. "Why, into a pirate. What else? How else can you climb the ropes?"

"Well, you just went into the history books as the coolest grandfather ever." Kimberly saw his mischievous smile when her father turned to face her. Her heart started to pound again and her eyes welled up. It was the same look he always gave her whenever they were about to do something special that Mom wasn't to know about. She had to swallow hard to get rid of the lump in her throat. Everything that had happened since they arrived brought back all the reasons why she missed him every day since he died. "What's that smile for? I know from experience that it can't be something good."

"I have a ladies pirate costume for you."

"Mom! Cool! You can climb up there with me!"

"Umm, no, I don't think so. I...I need to be down here in case you fall. I'll catch you."

"Lame, Mom, really lame." Peter shook his head as he started to dress in his pirate costume. "Can I keep this?"

"Gosh, Peter, you've been buying things left and right. I'll need a suitcase to take back with us. I don't know how Wolf is going to feel about that."

Her father adjusted the costume's red plumed hat to the proper rakish angle on Peter's head. "Now you look just like Captain Hook. But, I don't think the eye patch is a good idea. You'll need to watch where you put your feet."

"Aww." Peter reluctantly removed the item in question and handed it to his mom.

She promptly put it on. "How do I look?"

"Perfect." Her father shook his head as he looked at her. "I don't know how I'm going to wait for you to come along. I have a feeling we're going to have a wonderful time together."

"Yes, yes, we are. You're the best dad a girl could have."

"If you two start crying again, I'm leaving."

Kimberly dabbed quickly at her one eye that was showing. "You'll understand when you have kids of your own, Peter."

"Ewww."

She glanced at her father and sighed. "Which might be a lot longer away than we thought."

"Can I get into the rigging now?"

"Impatient little thing, isn't he, Kimberly?"

"Yeah. He's just like me."

"Oh, great. Now there's something else to look forward to." He motioned to the stairs. "Come on, Peter. Let's get you aloft."

"Oh, my stars. It looks so much taller from here. Are you sure…."

"Kimberly, the boy will be fine. Trust me."

"How come Walt didn't use forced perspective here and the mast is only a couple of feet tall?"

Kimberly just received a low chuckle for an answer. As Peter started his slow climb into the ropes, all conversation between them ceased.

"Steady, boy, hand over hand. Don't rush it. That's right. One step and then another." As he muttered the instructions to himself, Peter's grandfather found his heart rate had sped up as Peter got higher and higher. Three steps from the crow's nest, Peter missed his footing and his leg slipped through the rope.

Kimberly let out a terrified gasp when he floundered. A firm hand on her arm kept her from starting to climb herself.

"He's all right. See? He got his foot on the rope like it should be. He's fine."

"You sound a little breathless yourself, Daddy."

"There! He's in the crow's nest." He let out a breath he didn't realize he was holding. "It's different when it's someone else. Someone you…love. And don't start crying again."

Peter disappeared from view as he dropped into the crow's nest to find the hidden capsule. Heads up, both Kimberly and her father were so intent on the scene above they didn't hear someone come up behind them on the deck of the ship.

"Something I need to know about?"

At the familiar voice, Kimberly spun around.

"Walt! I mean, Mr. Disney. I...uh...."

"Don't hurt yourself, Kimberly. Walt, I'd like to introduce you to Kimberly Brentwood. That's Peter up in the crow's nest. He's following up on that clue you left."

Walt got a big smile across his face. "He is? Already? How could that be? We just got it into place. Er, nice to meet you, Kimberly."

"Shouldn't you be at Small World for the grand opening?"

Walt glanced sideways at his right-hand man. "You're supposed to be there with me. That's not for a couple of hours yet. Everything's all ready. So, are you and Peter from around here?"

Kimberly realized she was still wearing the eye patch when she noticed Walt's eyes go back to one side of her face. She hastily snatched it, only to have it tangle in her hair. "Oh, gosh." With a frustrated movement, she let it fall and knew it now dangled down her back. *Great first impression when I meet Walt Disney.* She remembered he just asked a question. "We're from, uh, Fullerton." Her mind started to race when she wondered if she revealed something she shouldn't.

If Walt noticed her nervousness, he didn't let on. "First time here?"

She threw a frantic look at her father. He gave her a quick nod. "You might say that," she managed to get out. At Walt's confused expression, she had to add something. "I mean, it is our first time on the Chicken of the Sea Pirate Ship. And Peter climbing the mast, of course."

They all heard a distracting yell and looked up to see Peter waving at them. Apparently he had found what he was searching for and began his ing evening. Say, let's go on the Mine Train. It's one of my favorites."

"You mean Big Thunder."

"No, I mean the Mine Train Through Nature's Wonderland."

"Is it a roller coaster?"

"Of course not. The Bobsleds are the only roller coaster in Disneyland."

"Oh. Then, no, thank you."

Kimberly stepped in and took the decision away from Peter. "I would love to see the Mine Train, Daddy. And, so will you, Peter."

They received an unenthused grunt for a reply as they retraced their steps through Sleeping Beauty Castle, the pirate costume now folded and stuffed into one of the bags of souvenirs Peter had already bought.

Fullerton — 1966

Wolf was extremely glad to see his boss again. The possible problem of him being an actual wolf and alarming Walt had quickly dissolved. Wolf reminded them that he had brought Dr. Claude Houser back in time in 1963 to visit Walt. The good doctor had found himself alone and at loose ends in the future. The trip back helped Claude get grounded and know all that had been done was for the good of Walt's legacy. From then on his work flourished. And Walt, for the first time, had seen Wolf's transformation.

Now, three years later, seated and relaxed in the living room that was familiar to everyone there, the eyes of three people and one wolf were glued on their guest.

After telling them about the New York World's Fair and the grand opening of Small World in Disneyland, Walt went on to something else near and dear to his heart.

"Say, Peter," he began with a twinkle in his eye. "Have you ever heard the story of Mowgli the Man Cub and Baloo the Bear?"

Before Peter could say he had seen the movie, Kimberly rushed in. "Yes, you've read the book by Kipling, *The Jungle Book*, haven't you, Peter?" She hoped he would take her lead as she smiled widely at him, willing him to understand what she meant.

Taking that as an affirmative, Walt went ahead with his story. "Well, that's what we've been working on. It's going to be one of the finest animated stories we've ever done. Let me tell you about it."

Walt stood from the sofa and began to slowly pace across the room. In that instant, he became Bagheera the panther who just found a baby boy in the jungle. As he stooped to pick up the bundle, Walt morphed into the she wolf who raised the man cub as her own.

The mood changed when evil Shere Khan was known to be in the jungle. Ever alert, Bagheera decided to take Mowgli to the Man Village for his safety. As darkness fell over the jungle, the snake Kaa came to Mowgli and hypnotized him. Walt was out of breath as the snake squeezed until Bagheera arrived to save the day.

An umbrella from the entry hall became the baton Colonel Hathi used to inspected his ranks of elephants. Cheeks blown out, Walt trumpted the elephant's call and marched around the sofa of rapt

CHAPTER 15

Fullerton — 1966

"It will be quiet around here when you're gone." The blonde-haired man watched his future daughter and grandson make their final preparations. Wolf had instructed them to make Peter's numerous packages as small as possible to take back through the portal. Since they would not be traveling through water, it was hoped all would arrive safely—people as well as souvenirs.

The man became silent as his mind replayed the unbelievable events of the day. The bits and pieces Kimberly and Peter had inadvertently revealed about the future were stored away in his mind. At some later point they would taken out one by one to be examined and dissected. What came to the forefront now, though, was what Kimberly had said about him as her father and their relationship. It gave him a twinge when he recalled that, quite often, her words were spoken in the past tense, as if he was no longer in the picture in her time. *When did it happen? Is there something I might do….*

In a daze, he walked over to the place where they had just vanished. Expecting to find a wide circle of trampled, scorched grass, all that remained was just one glowing pink ember. As he tentatively reached out to touch it with the toe of his shoe, it fizzled and went out.

He turned a full circle, looking, as if they might emerge from the trees with a laugh and say it was just an illusion. But, he knew better. They were safe in the future.

He knew they were safe. He knew in his heart that they had made it safely back. It couldn't be any other way.

With a heavy sigh, he returned to his living room. There was a wadded gift bag from Disneyland Peter had carelessly dropped on the floor. Bright yellow, it was covered with balloons and streamers. With infinite care, he smoothed out the wrinkles and set it on the table next to the sofa. His wallet was taken from his back pocket and he removed the two odd-looking twenties he had swapped with Peter. As he held them up to the light, he marveled at the holographic pictures he could see.

In spite of his despondency, a thought entered his mind and mixed in with the sadness. It began to light the darkness and gave him something he could do to reconnect with those who had just left. He glanced up at the ceiling as if he could see the War Room on the third floor. *They will live here. This is their house.*

A smile broke out on his face as he turned to go upstairs. The security code was punched into the small hidden panel next to the thick door. Without even seeing the map of Disneyland that hung in the middle of the room, he stood in the doorway and looked around. His eyes narrowed. *Where would they find it? What would they keep?*

Behind a picture on the wall? No, too obscure. The desk? Perhaps. The largest filing cabinet? Probably.

He sat at the desk and set the money and paper bag to the side. A sheet of monogrammed paper was taken from the top drawer. He tapped a pen against his lips as he thought and then began to write.

Fullerton — Current Day

"**W**e made it! We're home!"

Peter and Kimberly happily danced around the yard as Wolf slowly pulled on his security uniform. The weakness was still with him and he felt none of their exuberance. Once the last button was fastened, he sat heavily on the grass, mindless of the dew that seeped into the cloth.

A light came on in the kitchen and they could see the outline of someone peering out the window. Immediately the door flung open and Lance rushed out into the yard. He embraced his family while simultaneously trying to check and see if they were all right.

"I want to go text Catie and tell her what I got for her!"

With a laugh that revealed the anxiety and relief he felt, Lance put a restraining hand on Peter's

"That's how it works sometimes." Lance wrapped an arm around her waist. "I missed you and Peter."

"What about Michael and Andrew?"

"Oh, I didn't miss them at all."

She gave a light laugh and hit him in the arm. "How did you explain where Peter and I went? You didn't tell them about Wolf, did you?"

"Naw, they're too young for that. I told them you went to the mall."

"That they would believe. Wait until I tell you about Walt!"

"Tomorrow, honey, tomorrow. You need to sleep."

Kimberly tried to stifle a yawn. "But I'm not sleepy."

"Tell that to your pillow."

"You're really bossy, you know. My dad tried to warn me about you."

Lance smiled as they climbed the stairs. "Yeah, I know."

Alone in his room, too excited to sleep, Peter went to his closet and pushed aside a mass of dirty clothes on his closet shelf. A small metal box, well-worn and dented, was taken down and carefully carried to his bed. The lid squeaked as it was slowly lifted.

Over the years the box had been filled with treasures Peter had to hide from the eager, grabbing hands of his younger brothers. The top layers consisted of favorite marbles, a folded first-edition comic book, baseball cards, and a variety of keys that he would be hard-pressed to answer what locks they opened. To the casual observer, there was nothing to see of great value. To them. To Peter, though, the box—and each item inside—held a special meaning.

With a specific goal in mind, he pushed aside the memories of his younger years and paused when his eyes fell on the next layer of trinkets. Here were the memories of the treasure hunts from Walt Disney. There was the Gold Pass to Disneyland, the key that opened the mermaid, and hand-written notes from Walt, but he knew one very special item was missing—the Key to Disneyland. His mom had made sure to hide it again after his trip into the Haunted Mansion. Well, he had found it once already....

That's not what I'm looking for. Getting back to his original plan, Peter moved aside the paper items. On the very bottom of the box were the two items he had wanted to see again. He wasn't sure *why* he wanted to see them, but there was something that kept nagging at him in the back of his mind. In all the excitement of their return from the past, these two things seem to have been forgotten by everyone else.

Flashback — Galway, Ireland — 1948

"**W**here are we going, Walt? Is there another press conference?" Lillian looked around at the quaint shops and businesses that lined Quay Street. It didn't look like the usual places they went for the public announcements.

Walt tucked her arm deeper into his as they

walked along the sidewalk. "No, no, this is something different. I think I've talked about *The Little People* enough for one day. I'm still going to change the title, though.   It just doesn't seem...enough."

"Do any of your relatives live around here? We've had so many wonderful visits so far."

He gave her hand a pat as he searched for Thomas Dillon's store. "No, I'm looking for Number 1 Quay Street. It should be coming up pretty quick."

"I'm sure you'll tell me when you're ready." Lillian gave him a fond smile. She never knew where she would end up with Walt. Figuring it was probably a men's hat store, her eyes roamed the storefronts to see where she might like to go next.

"Here we are."

A bell tinkled over the door as they entered. Lillian was surprised to find herself in an elegant jewelry store. Walt tugged her arm and led her deeper inside.

"Ah, Mr. Disney. And Mrs. Disney. Right on time. What a pleasure. I'm the owner, Thomas Dillon. Now, how can I help you?"

Lillian shot a glance at Walt. He had a broad smile on his face. "Hello, Thomas. Yes, I'd like to see those rings I've heard so much about."

"Why don't we come back to our special guest room?   You'll be much more comfortable than standing at the counter. I'll ring for tea."

"Rings, Walt? What kind of rings?"

Thomas set a velvet-covered tray of bejeweled claddagh rings on the table in front of the Disney's. "You just take your time. I'll leave you two to discuss the rings."

As the owner of the store that had welcomed

Hollywood's most elite celebrities left, Lillian leaned toward the display. "Oh, Walt, they're lovely! It's so…perfect after we've spent so much time finding your Irish relatives! Oh, look at this one! What a lovely emerald."

"How about this one? There are diamonds circling the heart."

Lillian made her selection. "I would like this one. What about you?"

He slipped the ring onto the ring finger of her right hand. "Perfect fit! How about that? I like this one. Why don't you sit here and relax and enjoy your tea. I'll go see Thomas and take care of business."

Lillian held her right hand out in front of her to admire the ring. "Thank you, Walt. This means a lot!"

He smiled as he went out front to talk to the owner. Once their business was concluded, his choice was slipped onto his right hand. And a small parcel with two more rings was slipped into the pocket of his jacket.

Fullerton

Peter reached out a finger and traced the two hands that held the heart on the larger of the claddagh rings—the man's ring. He didn't know why it made him inwardly happy that the rings had been forgotten by everyone else. He just knew he wanted to keep them to himself and private. Something deep inside told him there would be a time in his future when these rings would be important to him and…. He paused in his thought and frowned. The smaller ring was a woman's ring.

"Gosh, I'm only thirteen. Why am I even thinking about that?" He shook his head as if to chastise himself, but the thought didn't leave his mind. "Well, whatever. They're safe."

With a glance at his closed bedroom door, he hurriedly replaced everything and put the box away. The rings were once again safely buried in the dark.

Early in the afternoon, alone in the War Room, Kimberly checked the holographic map of the Disney World to see if anything happened or may have been altered while she was in the past. She could see no differences in the flashing lights that indicated future finds for Walt's treasure hunts. The small hunt Peter and Catie were on had never been programmed into the system. She realized now that it had been a trial test for Walt to see how it would go and if he would do another.

The wall of monitors that relayed information from the Parks went through their rotations as she stared at them with unseeing eyes. Over and over, though, she found her mind had returned to their trip through time. With the realization that she needed to quit daydreaming and get some work done, she went to one of the filing cabinets to retrieve a file that now needed to be updated.

As she pulled the manila file folder from its slot, she noticed a large, unfamiliar envelope. She had been in and out of that particular cabinet for decades but had never seen it before. Wondering if Peter or Lance had hidden something, curiosity got the better of her and she pulled it out. Addressed to 'My Future Daughter,' Kimberly felt her heart rate speed up when she recognized the handwriting and the date on the upper edge—Saturday, May 28, 1966. It was from her father.

Eagerly she tore open the flap and upended the envelope. A yellow paper bag, some money and a letter fluttered to the desktop. With a curious frown, she looked over the two twenties. It was modern money, not something that had been put away for over fifty years. Then it hit her. "Peter's money! Dad swapped that with him."

"My darling daughter-to-be,

As I sit here in my War Room I try to imagine you sitting in this same place, holding this paper in your hands. I can see your beautiful face so clearly in my mind. Is that ugly floor lamp still in the corner? Hopefully you have made some needed changes to the sad décor in this important room!

It seems impossible that you were just here moments ago, you and Peter and the wolf. You, who haven't even been born yet. Why, I haven't even proposed to your mother! Perhaps I need to get busy with that. She's been waiting for me for a while now….

Yet, impossible as it seems, I know you were here. The small bits of physical evidence—that paper bag from Peter and that odd-colored money of yours—are what remained behind. And I wanted you to have them to remember me and our special time together.

Will I remember this adventure and talk to you about it when you are old enough? Will I go over it with Wolf as we continue to work together with Walt? How can I not remember this?

I don't know. It is all so…so bizarre.

Even though we just met, I wanted to tell you how proud I am of you. Yes, that does sound odd, doesn't it? But, you, of all people, will understand what I mean. Peter is such a fine boy. I will enjoy meeting him, too."

Kimberly dropped the letter onto the desktop and sighed. "Oh, Daddy, I wish that would have happened. I just couldn't tell you."

"You seem to be a wonderful mother. My heart swells with pride.

I won't keep you longer. With three boys you must be busy. I was glad, too, to know you are following in my footsteps. If you find this letter, then it really is true.

What a joy I have to look forward to. Thank you, and Wolf, for allowing this to happen. I know the thing Wolf does is horrifying. It took all I had not to snatch you and Peter away from that…that terrible portal. But, I also had to trust you and Wolf. I hope it was all worth it for you. It sure was for me!

Thank you again, and remember your dear old dad!"

"**H**ey, Peter, I have a surprise for you."

Still tired from too little sleep and a rough day at school, Peter didn't burst with anticipation at his mom's words. "Yeah? What is it?"

"You could at least act a *little* interested."

"I'm interested, Mommy!" Seated next to his brother, Andrew perked up as he ate his after-school snack. "I like surprises."

Kimberly gave her youngest a hug and slipped him a cookie. "Sorry, sweetie. This is something

Peter, uh, left behind and was found."

Thinking of lost socks or something else uninteresting, Andrew grabbed his cookie and headed out the back door.

Now Peter's interest was piqued. "What did you find? My skateboard?"

"You lost your skateboard! The new one we just got you?"

"Oops, uh, yeah. Didn't I tell you about that?"

"Don't try that charming smile on me, mister. We'll discuss that later." Now angry, Kimberly thrust out something to her son. The moment was spoiled. "Here."

The joy of the discovery that it was money was overshadowed by the lecture he knew would come when his dad got home. "Forty dollars? When did I lose forty dollars?"

"Now that I think about it, that might just pay for your skateboard. That's the money you exchanged with your grandfather at Disneyland. Remember? He kept it all those years and put it somewhere where I would find it. Now, hand it over."

Peter knew not to grumble. Out loud. He watched the money disappear back into his mother's pocket. "Well, that was nice of him. Even though I don't get to keep it."

The emotion of the letter overtook the anger and Kimberly's eyes teared up. "He also said what a fine boy you were and how proud he was of us. Wasn't that nice?"

"Mom...you're not going to cry again, are you?"

Boys. "No, I'm not going to cry again." *In public.* She knew it was time to switch topics. "Did you make arrangements with Catie to open the next clue?"

Peter nodded. "She says her parents would like to come over tonight so we can all do it together. If we need to go to Disneyland again, maybe we can go after we figure it out."

"I think Beth was working Pirates today. Maybe she, Lance and Wolf worked that out already."

"Do you think there will be more clues after this one, Mom?"

She had to shrug. "I don't know, honey. But I do know that we need to get all this sorted out before Grandma Margaret's three days are up—and that's almost here."

Peter looked at the rest of his snack and pushed it away. The threat of Omah that hung over their heads was enough to make him lose his never-ending appetite. "I...I hope everything will be all right." He paused and looked miserable as he chewed on his bottom lip. All his words spilled out in a rush. "I feel like it's my fault for all of this! If I hadn't found the mermaid, none of this would have happened. I...I don't want Grandma Margaret to get hurt."

"Oh, honey." Kimberly hadn't known Peter felt so strongly about the danger. She moved closer and enfolded him in her arms. "We'll just have to make sure you and Margaret and Catie are all fine. You have a lot of wonderful people looking out for you. You believe that, don't you?"

He snuggled into the hug and let his mother's warmth seep into him. They were both momentarily taken back to a time not so long ago when all of Peter's problems could be solved within his mother's arms. "Yeah. Wolf will take care of her!"

"Wolf is pretty awesome, all right. What time did you say they would be here?"

"I think they said around five."

The warm, fuzzy moment abruptly exploded. Kimberly jerked back and looked at the clock. "Five! You never said it was for dinner! That's in an hour!"

"Oh. Was that important?"

Ah, the oblivion of youth. Kimberly just shook her head and mentally counted to ten. *Could he be even more like his father? Was that even possible?* "So, what do you want? Pepperoni or sausage pizza?"

The talk at dinner revolved around Kimberly and Peter's trip. Peter had a good time passing out the souvenirs he had bought—items that, under normal circumstances, would have been worn out or dog-eared after all those years.

Beth set down the small round ceramic plate Peter had chosen for her. The elaborate Castle and the Matterhorn were in shades of white and gold set against the pale pink background of the plate. There was even an attached pink ribbon so it could be hung on the wall. "Peter, that's just lovely. Thank you."

He smiled with pleasure at her words. Everyone seemed to be happy with what he had chosen for them. Adam, the avid historian, loved the 1966 wall map of the Park and eyed Catie's unused ticket book with its admission ticket still attached. They knew Margaret would appreciate the ornate brass telephone dialer. Peter explained it was a replacement for the golden can opener Alex ruined when the first capsule had been opened. Michael received a small winding Mickey Mouse watch—so different from the battery-operated ones currently sold. Andrew was off in the corner drawing with the tall, four-colored pencil that had a rubber Pluto head on top. Alex was looking for a place to try out his Native American tomahawk from the Trading Post in Frontierland. When he saw Aunt Kimberly watching him like a hawk, he decided to put it back into the bag and try again later. Catie loved her small plastic snow globe filled with silver glitter. Inside, Donald Duck skippered a Jungle Cruise boat that tottered back and forth as she moved it. A brown monkey swung above the boat's roof.

"Hey! That's my old security badge! How did you…oh, never mind."

Lance ignored Wolf's glare as he pinned onto his shirt the badge his father-in-law had swiped for him. He patted it once it was in place and saw that all eyes were on him. "Well, that leaves just one thing to do. We need to open the capsule that was obtained at risk of life and limb. Peter, since you faced the danger like a man, I think you should open it."

There was a spontaneous round of applause as Peter got to his feet and took a bow. His green eyes sparkled as he eyed the gray plastic held out to him. "Yes, sir. Alex, can I borrow your tomahawk?"

"No!"

Peter gave a laugh. "Just kidding. I already loosened the cap."

He shot a glance at his dad when he heard "Excuse me?"

"Well, I knew we were going to do this and I didn't want to hold everyone up."

"Always thinking of others, son. So, what's in it?"

Peter gave a grin as he easily pulled the end cap off. "I didn't open it, Dad. I'm not selfish, you know." His smile faded when the expected accolades of his integrity did not immediately come forth. "Well, I'm not. Fine." He gave a big sigh and up-ended the capsule. A large brass key fell out.

"Careful, Peter! That might be fragile." Adam dove for the key as it slid across the coffee table. "Oh, its solid brass. Never mind. I think it scratched your table, Kimberly. Wow, look at that design! The bow looks like it has a Hidden Mickey carved out of the brass." He ran his fingers down the elaborate shank. "This looks like a one-of-a-kind piece of work. The key ward—or, you might call them teeth—have a lot of carving and cuts." He held it up for them to see. "There's only one lock this key will fit. I have a feeling that's where this clue will lead…. There is a clue in there, isn't there, Peter?"

Now that Uncle Adam's lecture on keys was over, Peter looked inside the small capsule. "Yeah, there's a piece of paper rolled inside. I got it!" His face screwed up a little as he looked at the diary paper. "Oh. It's another poem. Here, you read it." He thrust the note to Catie, who was more than happy to see what it said and read it aloud to the group:

"Mermaids are stuff of legends.
Folk tales, yarns, and lore.
In my mind they are beautiful.
You met a few. There are more.

This Mermaid's Tale is finished.
Your daring feats are done.

There's one last place to send you.
I hope you've had some fun.

Remember me tomorrow that's
Shining at the end of ev'ry day.
I hope you like your treasure.
Like me, you have a place to stay.

106 Main Street."

They all started talking at once.

"What does he mean you have a place to stay?"

"What's at 106 Main Street? I'm not familiar with the numbers."

"This sounds to me like this will be the last clue."

"Is there any more pizza?"

"Can we go to Disneyland now and check it out?"

"You think this key fits whatever is at that address?"

"Mom! Sunnee just peed in the kitchen."

"Do Catie and I get to keep what we find or do we have to share it?"

A loud, piercing whistle caused everyone to cover their ears. All eyes turned to the originator, Wolf. He had been quietly standing in the corner listening all evening. When the noise got to be too much, he put an end to it. "Now that I have your attention, why don't we talk about the one thing that's the most important?"

Peter held up the key he had gotten back from Adam. "This?"

"I think it's the poem." Catie blushed when all

eyes turned to her. "Well, it does tell us where we need to go. Wherever that is...."

"I think we need to get the directory and find out what's at 106 Main Street."

Wolf shook his head and sighed. "No, Adam. That's not what I meant. I think we need to discuss the mermaid and Omah. The three days are up tomorrow. Do you want your mom to have to face that woman alone while we're at Disneyland?"

The reality of the situation smacked Adam in the face. "You're right. I, for one, have been selfishly enjoying this Hidden Mickey quest and forgot all about Omah. I guess I lost track of time."

"Can't you take care of her, Wolf?"

"What would you like me to do, Peter?"

At Wolf's pointed question, Peter had to stop and think. He didn't expect to have to figure it out himself. "I dunno. You fix everything."

"Well, sometimes I do. But this is different. Other than vague threats and, well, throwing a knife at you, she hasn't done anything yet. Yet," he stressed. He turned back to Adam. "Your mom says she only wants the mermaid the kids found in the attic. Is that the way you understood it? That she isn't interested in the clue trail?"

Adam had to shrug. "Yeah, that's the way I see it, too." He looked around the group. "Did she say anything else to any of you that showed this isn't true? That she wants nothing more than the mermaid?"

Peter's face fell. "You mean I have to give her up? Well, what about the pearls? Can I keep those? She never seemed to be interested in them."

"You're right, Pete. The pearls have never

been mentioned." Lance lifted a shoulder as he thought. "I don't see why not. We'll figure them out later to see if there is some connection to the mermaid."

"Thanks, Dad."

Wolf came over to the boy and put a hand on his shoulder. "I think giving up the mermaid might solve everything. You have a lot of other things you and Catie have gotten—including those pearls and the promise of something else on Main Street. We're talking about getting rid of a nuisance. There won't be any more threats to Grandma Margaret— or Catie and you. Isn't it worth it?"

Already sitting next to Peter, Catie put a hand on his arm. "I think Wolf is right. I hate to see the mermaid go, too, but I...I don't want to be afraid every time I go to Disneyland any more."

"I didn't know you were afraid, Catie." Peter looked down at the small hand on his arm. He began to feel guilty for making a fuss about the mermaid. "Let's go take the mermaid to Grandma Margaret. We can all be there when that woman comes back."

Wolf and the other adults in the room gave a nod. "Good choice, Peter."

Chapter 16

Yorba Linda

"As happy as I am to see all of you, why aren't you two in school?" Margaret gave her granddaughter and Peter a hug. She looked a little surprised when Adam and Beth, Lance and Kimberly, and Wolf all trooped in through her front door. "No Alex and the boys? To what do I owe this honor?" With a smile she accepted a bright yellow paper bag that Peter held out to her. "What's this?"

"It's a replacement for the can opener that we broke when we opened the gray capsule. I couldn't find the exact same thing, so I hope you like it."

Margaret looked at the bright gold of the rotary phone dialer and knew it had to have come back with Peter through time—however that worked…. "So, your…trip was successful?"

Kimberly put a hand on Peter's shoulder. She could tell he was about to launch into a lengthy dissertation of their trip. "Yes, it went really well. We'll tell you all about it later. Is, uh, John here?"

Knowing what she meant, Margaret shook her

head. "It's okay to talk. He's at the home improve-
ment store." Then, hands clasped together, she
asked what was closest to her heart, her eyes shining. "So, did you get to visit with your dad? Was it
wonderful?"

Thinking only of what his dad might be doing
next, Adam looked around the living room. "What's
he working on now? The place looks perfect."

Margaret took Adam's interruption in stride.
With a wink to Kimberly, she mouthed the words
'we'll do lunch soon and talk.' "The place looks perfect to you, Adam, but not to your dad. You know
how he loves to putter ever since he turned the construction company over to you. I think we're getting
a new pond out back."

"Well, we wanted to be here just in case Omah
comes back. This is the day she said she would."

The fond smile faded at Lance's words and
Margaret gave a heavy sigh. She had been desperately trying not to think of it. "I'm still hoping
she'll forget and not show up. You think it's necessary for *all* of you to be here? You think she's that
much of a threat?" Peter's movement caught her
eye and she saw him take the mermaid in question
out of his backpack. "So, you decided to let her
have it?"

"I'd like to let her have it…." Wolf looked up
when suddenly all eyes turned to him. "Did I say
that out loud? Sorry."

"That's okay." Adam silently agreed with him.
"We know how you feel, Wolf. Yes, Mom, we
thought it'd be best. We want to question her first.
You know, make sure this is all she wants and that
she won't be back. That sort of thing."

Margaret looked at the worried faces of Peter

and Catie. Her maternal, grandma instinct kicked in and she felt she needed to do something to lighten the mood. "Say, since this seems to be I-didn't-have-to-go-to-school Day, why don't we have a nice picnic out by the pool? You two kids come with me and we'll fix something special for lunch. How does that sound? I made a nice pumpkin bread for Grandpa John that he won't mind sharing."

Lance looked up from his plateful of food. "I hope this won't take too long. We need to get to Main Street. Say, where's Wolf? He didn't leave, did he?"

"I think he stationed himself by the front door. He doesn't want Omah to surprise us."

"Now wasn't that selfish of him. I thought everyone liked surprises."

Everyone startled at the sarcastic, superior voice of Omah as she walked around the far edge of the pool.

"How did you get in here?" Adam immediately stood to challenge her as he stepped in front of his wife and daughter.

Kimberly took the moment of diverted attention to shoo the kids inside. "Go in the house, honey. Peter, let Wolf know we have a visitor, won't you? And then stay put!"

Omah extended a hand and tried to approach Kimberly. "I don't think we've been properly introduced. I'm...."

"I know who you are." Kimberly's words were calm but pointed as she folded her arms over her chest. She did not want to shake hands with this woman.

Adam took a step closer to Omah. "I think you can stay right where you are. We need to talk."

She looked Adam up and down. "This is your boy, Margaret? I see the resemblance to John. How…sweet."

Before anyone could respond, Wolf stormed through the patio door. "We need to talk, Omah."

Amused, she looked from Adam to Wolf. "Is there an echo in here? I don't think you all rehearsed who should say what. This could get boring if everyone keeps repeating themselves."

Wolf pointed to an empty patio chair. "Sit."

"Arf." Omah grinned at her joke but chose to remain where she was, her blue eyes narrow as they stared back at Wolf.

They could all see him grind his teeth. He wasn't one for pleasantries. "Would you have a seat so we can discuss the matter?"

"Why, thank you. I think I will." With a grand flourish, she settled into the chair as a queen onto her throne. "Now, what is there really to discuss? I want my mermaid. Where is it?"

Adam put a restraining hand on Wolf's arm to indicate he would take over for now. Wolf took one, small step back, his only concession. "Now that we are all comfortable, we can begin." Out of the corner of his eye, Adam saw a movement and glanced at the patio door. Peter and Catie used the curtains as a shield as they watched and listened to the proceedings. "I will first off say that we do have the mermaid here." He held up a hand when Omah was about to rise from the chair. "I'm not done."

She sank back and glared at him. "Then get on with it. Now that I know you all have become reasonable, I have someplace to go."

"In due time. As I said, we brought the mermaid as you...requested. What we want to make perfectly clear is that, once you have the mermaid, you will never again approach any of us. Not Lance or Kimberly. Not me. Not Margaret. And especially not any of the children. We don't want to see you or even hear your name mentioned. Is that clear? Is that understandable?"

Omah looked up from working on a cuticle with an extremely sharp nail file she had pulled out of her jacket's pocket. "Oh, you're done? Is that all? Anything else I should 'understand'?"

"Put that away."

Omah looked at the nail file and then held it up for Wolf to see. "Oh, I'm sorry. Are you afraid of my nail file? Good thing I didn't bring scissors. You might have had a heart attack."

If it had been possible, Wolf would have gotten angrier. Lance put a hand on his friend's shoulder. "I am not afraid of you. Enough of this." Lance's hand was roughly pushed away. He stalked over to the chair where he was regarded with a cool, even stare. "You will make the promise and leave, or...."

"Or what? We're just having a nice chat here. Is he always this impetuous?"

"Do not toy with me, woman. You have threatened the children and scared people that I care about. And this needs to end now!"

"Threaten?" She looked genuinely taken aback. "How in the world did I threaten the darling children?"

"You threw a knife at them."

"Oh, that." A manicured hand airily waved him off. "I missed, didn't I?" Her eyes narrowed as she looked up at the imposing Wolf who still stood over her. "And I never miss. I always hit what I aim at. Don't forget that."

Margaret had had enough of this and took a step forward. She could tell Wolf was just about to burst a vein in his neck. Cooler heads needed to prevail. "Omah, all we want is the promise that you will take the mermaid and leave us alone." She tried to appeal to the woman's reasonable side—if she had one. "You and I had some fun together as mermaids at Disneyland a long time ago. I'd rather have that memory of you than this one."

As Omah looked over at Margaret, her expression seemed to soften a little. "All I wanted was the mermaid. I tried to ask nicely, but that didn't work."

"Why do you want it so badly? We can't figure that part out."

Beth received a sharp glance when Omah abruptly stood from her chair. The easier moment Margaret had created vanished. Angry again, she paced back and forth across the deck as she talked, her words spilling out in a heated rush. "What difference does that make to you people? I thought I made it clear. I have to give it back to…someone. It was part of a test and I failed when it was stolen and I couldn't find it. I have to prove I'm not a failure. Now give me my mermaid and I will leave you alone!"

The adults all exchanged looks as Omah stopped and just stood there, her breathing rapid and uneven. Surely she had to know Walt had been gone all those years. Was she mad? Had the decades-long search deranged her mind? Would she keep her promise to stay away once she realized Walt would never know she retrieved the mermaid?

Peter came slowly through the patio door, the red-headed mermaid held carefully in his hands. Catie followed a moment later.

"Son…."

"Its okay, Dad. It has to go to her. It won't get any better if it doesn't."

Omah whirled around at the sound of Peter's voice. In her haste, she dropped the nail file. As she stooped to retrieve it, eyes only on the boy, the sharp edge was unknowingly held out in front of her as Peter approached.

"Stop her!"

"Ouch!"

"Peter, get back!"

With a clumsy movement, Omah had grabbed the mermaid from Peter and quickly turned on her heels. She was only four steps ahead of Wolf as she raced for the stand of trees at the back of the yard.

The rest of the adults pushed the children back into the house.

"We need to help Wolf!"

"Wolf can take care of himself, Peter. Did she hurt you? Did she stab you?"

"I don't know. My finger's bleeding. Musta been when she grabbed the mermaid."

"He's all right." Her heart pounding, Kimberly looked her son over and then examined the cut. Relieved, she could tell it was just a scrape. "I don't want to believe this was intentional."

As one, they all turned when the patio door jerked opened. A glowering Wolf stood there, his hair covered with leaves. "She got away."

"What do you mean she got away? Where is

Adam received a half-smile from Lance. "Does he ever?"

"True."

Kimberly and Beth hung back as the kids ran back and forth across Main Street. Not all the buildings had addresses, so they had to use deductive reasoning to figure out which one should be number 106.

"This reminds me of the hunt Lance and I were on together." Kimberly tilted her head. "We ended up on the porch with the chairs up another block. There's a secret stairway between the silhouette store and the cast member lockers."

"I remember you told us about that. How did you get inside the building, though? There are always people sitting there."

Kimberly gave a fond smile. It had been a special time for her. She and Lance had fallen in love during that quest. He had been a big support when she suddenly lost her dad. "We waited for the fireworks. One minute we were there, then, boom! The lights went out and we were gone!"

"Smart." Beth leaned back against the building that housed the Magic Shop. "It's amazing what we come up when we have to. Adam had to slosh through the water flume of Pirate's to get what we needed. My, that was a long time ago. Adam and I got reconnected during our treasure hunt."

Kimberly watched Peter and Catie as Peter pointed up to the number 107 on the Crystal Arcade across the street. She gave a secret smile. "Yeah, it looks like Walt's little quests have that affect on a lot of people."

The kids ran north on Main Street and stopped in front of the Market House. Peter jotted the number down in his little notebook and they came tearing back. "Mom! That's number 122, so it's down too far. It has to be closer to here since the Arcade is 107."

There was a short staircase next to their location lit by an acorn-shaped light fixture. Only four steps tall, it ended at a brown door in the cream-colored inlet. People could be seen the in windows of the shops of either side, but this place had the air of abandonment. Peter stepped back to look up at the upper story. One tall rounded window was set between two rectangular ones. Lace curtains hid the interior as they looked out over the busy street.

"I think this is the place."

"But, if the door did open, it looks like it would go into the back part of the Market House, Peter. And it doesn't look like it's ever been opened."

"I know, Catie, that's why it's perfect!"

Peter ran up the short flight of stairs. When he examined the round brass doorknob, he immediately saw there was no keyhole. He put a hand on the knob and gave it a light twist. It didn't move. "There's no place to put the key."

"Maybe we need to go inside the Magic Shop."

With a light jump, he bypassed the steps and landed on the walkway. "But that address is 102 Main Street. No, I think this is it. Mom?"

Kimberly held up her hand. "This is your quest. You two will figure it out."

Peter turned back to the small inlet. It was only about four feet wide. "Why would there be a mailbox if it wasn't a real place? Why is it up so high?"

CHAPTER 17

Disneyland

"**A** ladder? We have to climb a ladder?"

The two women found themselves squeezed into a dark, narrow, closet-sized space. Catie's feet had already vanished above them and they could hear the kid's muffled, excited voices.

Beth grasped the first rung of the cold metal. "Just pretend we're at the gym. Now we won't have to work out for a while!"

"I hate going to the gym." Kimberly gave a sigh. She and Lance had scaled Tarzan's Treehouse in their quest. One ladder shouldn't stop her. Beth's voice now mingled with the children's as they explored what she could not see. "Fine. Don't wait for me."

As if she had heard Kimberly's mumbled comment, Beth's face appeared at the top of the ladder. "Aren't you coming? You're not going to believe this!"

Kimberly's eyes grew wide as she pulled herself up the last rungs. If she hadn't known better, she would have sworn she was in Walt's apartment over the Fire Station across Main Street. "This is amazing."

Peter and Catie ran from one piece of furniture to the next as they pulled off the covering sheets. In their excitement, their moms guessed they probably didn't even realize what they had uncovered.

"Slow down, you two! What do you make of this?"

"Mom, Walt left us an apartment just like his!" Peter happily threw himself onto the Victorian armchair set in the middle of a red, floral rug. His blonde hair was haloed by dust in the dusky light that filtered in through the lace curtains.

Beth stifled a sneeze. "Hope Walt left a vacuum…. Let's take these covers off a little more slowly, please. Who knows how long they've been in place. Catie, help me with this one. It's pretty big."

The next piece that emerged from its shroud was a red velvet sofa flanked by two lovely antique tables. If the furniture did mirror what was in Walt's apartment, it would probably be a sleeper sofa.

Kimberly emerged from the back of the apartment. "There's a tiny bathroom and shower back there. This really is an apartment!"

"And it's ours! We can stay overnight at Disneyland any time we want to!"

"Mom, can we…."

"No, it's a school night." Beth pulled open a set of white folding doors. "Here's a small kitchenette. Look, there's even a two-slice toaster. This is so…so cool!" She turned a full circle and compared what she was seeing to what she remembered about Walt's apartment. "This is really close to what Walt's place looks like. The furniture isn't exactly the same, though. Close, but I can tell these are reproductions while Walt's are true antiques."

"There aren't any pictures on the wall or any thingys on the tables like at home."

Kimberly nodded at Peter's observation as she looked around. "Probably because Walt figured whoever found it would want to decorate it them-selves."

Catie called them over. "Hey, look at this! It was in the closet. It's heavy."

"What is it?"

Beth looked over their shoulders as Catie set the item on the coffee table. "That looks like brass. Why would he leave a flower arrangement?"

"Remember, Beth? There used to be a flower market just a few steps from here on East Center Street."

Beth wasn't listening. Intent on the item and a piece of trivia in the back of her mind, she wanted to see the vase. "It's so oddly shaped. Would you mind if I take out the flowers?" Since Peter and Catie were the new owners of the apartment, she directed the question to them.

The two kids just shrugged. "I guess."

"Oh, my!" Beth's hand went to her mouth as the vase was completely revealed. "I heard about this years ago. I never thought I'd get to see it."

"It's a hat."

Beth had to smile at the unenthused tone of Peter's voice. "Not just a hat. This was one of Walt's fedoras! Come sit on to the sofa and I'll tell you about it." She saw the look exchanged by the two kids. "Hey, it won't take that long. Come and sit."

"Well, I'm curious, even if they're not. What's the story, Beth?"

Happy to dig into her vast knowledge of Disney history, Beth ignored Peter's bored expression. "Walt and Lillian had a friendly, long-running argument over the hats Walt wore. He loved them all crumpled up and she didn't like the ones he always chose to wear. When Lillian would ask him to please fix his hat, he would literally crush it onto his head and pull it at a sharp angle over his forehead. There was even an incident after a bull fight. Once it was over, Lillian didn't say a word but tossed his hat into the ring as a tribute to the fighters. Since it was one of his favorites Walt ran down and rescued it before it could be trampled and lost forever." Beth stopped and grinned. She loved these hat stories.

"Once she even pulled his hat off his head and tossed it out of the convertible they were driving in. He had to stop the car to run back and get it. He crammed it back on his head and they went on their way." Beth went back to the table and picked up the bronze hat. "Then, later, in 1941, Walt did something very special. He had the brim of that same hat—this one—shaped into a heart and had the whole thing bronzed. It was filled with violets and given to Lillian as a present. This is that present."

"Aww, that's so sweet."

Beth smiled at her daughter. "I thought you'd like it, Catie."

"Gosh, one more story like that and I'll cry."

Startled, their heads jerked toward the ladder opening. Omah pulled herself into the room and looked around the apartment, ignoring the startled faces around her. "So this is what he did." Walt had never shown her the final prize. The muttering continued as she stalked over to the window and jerked it open. "So greedy to see what they got that they don't even let some fresh air in."

"What are you doing here!? You promised to stay away. How did you find us?"

The sharp blue eyes narrowed at Kimberly as Omah came to the center of the room. "So many questions. So few answers you deserve. If you don't want people to know you're going to Main Street, don't announce that you're going to Main Street."

"I don't care how you found us. Get out! Keep away from us!"

Her attention focused on Beth. "Do not tell me what to do." She suddenly turned and pointed at Peter who took a step back. "And you! You ruined everything!"

They could see a glint of silver from her hand. Not knowing if the angry woman was armed, Beth stood in front of the children. "Get out and get out now. Wolf will be here any moment."

"Wolf." The word was almost spat out. "I've watched you ever since you got here. No sign of your precious Wolf." Her attention went back to the startled boy. "You had to butt in and spoil it. He…he said nothing mattered since you figured out the clue anyway. It didn't matter if I got the mermaid back or not! You ruined it!"

"Who are you talking about?" Kimberly's heart had started to pound in her chest. They all had assumed Wolf was watching from the shadows. She felt she needed to keep this woman talking so she couldn't act on what she obviously came to do.

"Who said it didn't matter? Who are you talking about?"

"Wal…It's none of your business who I mean. I have a score to settle with the boy."

"You will not touch my son!"

The silver dropped lower and the edge of a blade was clearly visible. "I will do what I want."

"Get away from the boy!" Wolf's deep voice came from the opening in the floor.

Omah spun around to face the angry security guard as he jumped into the room. "He ruined my life."

"He did nothing. This is your own doing, Omah. Drop the knife."

"That boy doesn't deserve this prize. I want that key so he can never come back here again."

"You get nothing." Wolf slowly walked toward the woman, his glare boring into her.

Eyes wide, she backed away, knowing the small blade in her hand would not stop him. It took only one look around the room to reveal how she would get away. Wolf had the access to the ladder blocked. That left only one other exit.

With a sudden, fluid movement, she flung herself out the open window. Knowing it was there—and her only way out—the awning over the stairs broke her fall. With a bounce and the agility of an acrobat, she grabbed the edge of the awning and swung down onto Main Street. A crowd of startled, gaping onlookers scrambled out of her way.

Wolf flew down the ladder and quickly hit the hidden latch. As the door flew open, he ran out to the sidewalk. Looking both ways, unsure which way she had gone, several guests pointed north on Main Street. As he took off, he finally spotted her close to the buildings, pushing people out of her way as she ran.

She knew she would be followed, but she also knew exactly where she was headed. Her breathing wasn't even labored as she rounded the Matterhorn and ran past the Submarine Lagoon.

Wolf started to gain ground as he pursued the woman. She wasn't going to get away this time.

At the far end of the Motor Boat Cruise dock, Omah stopped and turned to wait. It would be only moments before Wolf would reach her. With a sneering smile on her face, she knew exactly what she was going to do.

Expecting the dock to be empty, Wolf came to a skidding halt when he saw Omah standing at the end. He could tell by her arrogant stance that she was waiting for him. There were a few people sitting on the benches under the Monorail track who eyed them curiously. It took only a word from the angry security guard to send them elsewhere.

Once they were alone, Wolf slowly neared her position. "You aren't going to get away this time, Omah. You won't get past me again."

"Only a fool goes into a place with just one exit. And I am no fool. Don't think for a moment that you have the upper hand, Wolf."

His blue eyes narrowed as he approached. It made him a little concerned that she was unafraid. People who think they have complete control can be the most dangerous. He knew to proceed with caution. "I am always in control, Omah."

She gave a low, uncaring chuckle. "You have

no idea what I can do, Wolf. No idea." She tilted her head to one side as she scrutinized him as if he was a bug under a glass. "You have this air about you. Tell me something, Wolf. What's your real name?"

That was not a question he expected. His pace slowed. She made no move to get away or showed any consternation that he was almost upon her. "That isn't important. This must end, Omah. You will not be allowed to scare and threaten the children again."

Arms folded across her chest, she ignored his warning. "Tell me your name. Or shall I guess?"

"It doesn't matter what you do."

The words were hissed. "Sumanitu Taka? Is that right, wolf?"

That stopped him in his tracks. No one outside of his closest friends knew his Lakota name. "So you are clever and figured out my heritage. So what? That doesn't change what will happen here."

"You have no authority over me, wolf."

Her superior attitude got the better of him. "You will not be allowed to just walk away."

"Aren't you even a little curious about *my* name? Omah is just part of it. Would you like to hear the rest?"

"I don't care what your name is." He was within a couple of feet from her. If they had both extended their hands they could have touched.

"My, how angry you are. I can feel your hands around my throat, squeezing."

"I haven't touched you!"

"But you would like to. Are you that violent, wolf? Is that what you have planned?"

She was trying to goad him into action. He

could feel it but stood where he was, assessing his options.

She smiled at his silence. "Since you asked so nicely, I shall tell you." Sarcasm dripped from her words. "My name is Omahkapi'si."

It took a full minute for the word to register with him. His breath came more rapidly as he stared at her. "That's a Blackfoot word. It means…wolf."

Her eyes glared at him and the knife dropped from her sleeve into her waiting hand. "Yes, it does. What are you going to do about it, wolf?"

In a split second he saw the knife come straight at him. With the agility of his namesake, he jumped aside. When it was heard hitting the dock with a metallic clang, he gave a roar and leaped at the woman.

Eyes flashing in anger, she snarled at him, "So, you want to play rough, do you? I'll show you rough!"

Arms around her slender frame, the two adversaries fell over the blue railing. Wolf closed his eyes and held his breath, expecting to hit the water at any moment.

With the awareness that came from centuries of travel, Wolf could feel the change come over him. It was the frantic, unwanted realization of a moment and then, the transformation into a wolf was complete.

There was no water beneath the two as they hit hard ground and rolled over. Legs still entwined around Omah, he refused to let go.

Wolf's eyes flew open when he heard an angry

growl and felt hot breath on his face.

He was no longer wrapped around the body of a woman.

He stared into the eyes of a large, snapping red wolf.

—THE END—

COMING IN 2015

HIDDEN MICKEY

ADVENTURES 4

REVENGE OF THE WOLF

NANCY TEMPLE RODRIGUE

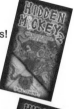

HIDDEN MICKEY MERCHANDISE ITEMS

 HIDDEN MICKEY COFFEE MUGS

BASEBALL CAPS FOR GROUP QUESTS

 SHIRTS FOR GROUP QUESTS

HIDDEN MICKEY JACKETS

 HIDDEN MICKEY CLOCKS

HIDDEN MICKEY SPECIALTY ITEMS

LIMITED EDITION
HIDDEN MICKEY HEART PENDANT
COPYRIGHT © 2010 BY NANCY RODRIGUE

AND MUCH MORE...
AVAILABLE AT:
WWW.HIDDENMICKEYBOOK.COM

JOIN THE HIDDEN MICKEY FAN CLUB AND GAIN ACCESS TO OUR ARCHIVED NEWSLETTERS WITH BEHIND-THE-SCENES ARTICLES WRITTEN BY PAST AND PRESENT CAST MEMBERS WITHIN THE DISNEY PARKS. FANS ALSO RECEIVE ADVANCE ANNOUNCEMENTS ON BOOK SIGNINGS, SPECIAL EVENTS, AND SPECIAL PURCHASE OPPORTUNITIES FOR NEW BOOKS AND MERCHANDISE BEFORE THESE ARE RELEASED TO THE PUBLIC.

HIDDEN MICKEY FAN CLUB:
www.HIDDENMICKEYBOOK.com/fanclub

FACEBOOK USERS CAN ALSO JOIN THE HIDDEN MICKEY FAN CLUB ON FACEBOOK. SIMPLY "LIKE" THE "HIDDEN MICKEY FAN CLUB" TO BE ENTERED IN THE BOOK GIVEAWAY CONTEST. EVERY TIME THE MILESTONE OF 50 "LIKES" IS REACHED, THE AUTHOR WILL GIVE AWAY A HIDDEN MICKEY ADVENTURES QUEST AND GAME BOOK TO A FAN CLUB MEMBER. JOIN TODAY TO WIN!

HIDDEN MICKEY FAN CLUB ON FACEBOOK:
www.FACEBOOK.com/HIDDENMICKEYFANCLUB

ABOUT THE AUTHOR

NANCY TEMPLE RODRIGUE

Nancy lives in the small town of Lompoc, California.

Her works show her admiration and respect for the man who started it all–Walt Disney. Her love of all things Disney was shown in her first four *Hidden Mickey* novels. Now, this new *Hidden Mickey Adventures* series features more action-adventures starring Wolf and the next generation of clue-solvers.

Hidden Mickey Adventures 1: Peter and the Wolf and this second book, *Hidden Mickey Adventures 2: Peter and the Missing Mansion* were written for all her readers to enjoy–Adults, Teens & Tweens (9 to 90). Now *Hidden Mickey Adventures 3: The Mermaid's Tale* continues the adventure.

See your favorite Disney Parks in a whole new way with Nancy's new *Hidden Mickey Quests* series. Find Hidden Mickeys and more by taking these quest books into the Parks. The games and quests take readers on a new and exciting journey.

Nancy actively holds book signing and speaking events. Visit www.hiddenmickeybook.com to follow the author's blog and learn the locations and dates of her book signing events. "Like" the Fan Club at www.FaceBook.com/HiddenMickeyFanClub

HIDDEN MICKEY ADVENTURES 3

The Third novel in this Action-Adventure Mystery series about Walt Disney and Disneyland, written for all ages (9 and up).

From the author of the acclaimed HIDDEN MICKEY series.

A FORGOTTEN TREASURE REVEALS A MISSING PUZZLE PIECE

Going through family mementos in their grandparent's attic, twins Alex and Catie Michaels, along with Peter Brentwood, stumble upon a familiar grey capsule—and pictures from Margaret Michaels' past

GRANDMA MARGARET WAS A MERMAID?

Thrilled to learn she was a Disneyland Submarine Lagoon Mermaid in 1965, they suddenly connect the missing link to the beautiful mermaid Peter and Catie found in the Haunted Mansion attic.

A MYSTERIOUS WOMAN HAS TO PROVE HERSELF

Given a simple assignment by her boss, Walt Disney, Omah was unable to complete it and sent away in disgrace. Decades later she is still trying to make it right, but three kids are in the way.

HER DEDICATION TURNS FANATICAL

Walt's Disneyland—then and now—is the backdrop of this exciting Mermaid's Tale. Pieces of the puzzle finally fall into place as three diverse groups are woven together in the past and the present—all of them determined to protect Walt Disney's legacy.

ALL 3 COLLIDE AS THE MERMAID'S TALE CONTINUES…

THE MERMAID'S TALE